D1177893

"YOU CAN'T BE BLUE AT SMILIN' THROUGH!"

That was the official camp song! And you'd better believe it: there simply wasn't time. Not with one counselor called The Hulk, another getting ready to run in the Boston Marathon, and a third trailing you with Cosell commentary. Not with a choice of baseball or canoeing or leaf-printing class or *e'se*! Not with Dance Nights and Field Days, pranks and pup tents and path-finding, with sneaking off into the woods with the Hardy Boys (if you were a boy) and combing the woods for a reading boy (if you were a girl). Not if you were an inner-city orphan faced with fresh air and the Ghost of Crazy Wilson for the first time in your life. No, there just wasn't time for the blues at Smilin' Through!

IF YOU'VE EVER BEEN TO SUMMER CAMP —AND EVEN IF YOU HAVEN'T . . .

Don't Miss

SUMMER CAMP

SUMMER CAMP

RICHARD WOODLEY

A Dell Book

Published by
Dell Publishing Co., Inc.
1 Dag Hammarskjold Plaza
New York, New York 10017

This novelization is based on the screenplay
by Michael Norell.

Copyright © 1979 by Dell Publishing Co., Inc.

All rights reserved. No part of this book may be reproduced or
transmitted in any form or by any means, electronic or mechani-
cal, including photocopying, recording or by any information
storage and retrieval system, without the written permission of
the Publisher, except where permitted by law.

Dell ® TM 681510, Dell Publishing Co., Inc.

ISBN: 0-440-18331-6

Printed in Canada

First Printing—April 1979

CHAPTER
1

Two battered yellow charter buses wheezed to a stop side by side next to the grass at one end of the shopping center parking lot. The two drivers sighed like the dying engines as they turned off the ignitions and sat looking across the asphalt.

Beside the buses was a hand-lettered cardboard sign nailed to a wooden pole that was planted in the grass. The sign read: BUSES FOR CAMP SMILIN' THROUGH.

Directly ahead in line with the drivers' vision was an array of smaller signs on smaller poles held up by Christmas tree stands. The signs identified Indian tribes: Cheyenne, Penobscot, Hopi, Cherokee, Seminole, Navajo, Iroquois, Choctaw, Mohawk, Sioux.

But the signs didn't *really* identify Indian tribes, of course. Under the tribal names were listed the names of the campers belonging to each cabin. Children and counselors who milled and danced and hopped and hollered and pushed around the signs, however, could have been involved in some historic dance of war or celebration.

That was why the drivers sighed. Indians would be a whole lot easier to haul.

The confusion of the lining-up process was heightened by the presence of parents, some reluctant to leave their offspring for the three weeks in the woods, some trying to extricate themselves from the grasps and beseeching looks of children reluctant to be left.

The parents, now gradually leaving, were more or

less the same size, though their ages ranged from the twenties to the fifties. But the children they left, though at ages only between eight and thirteen, were of vastly different sizes, some seemingly double the bulk of others. And again unlike the parents, who though of slightly differing moods acted more or less the same, the children evinced a mood range from tears to boisterous laughter, from passive or nervous standing to wrestling and back-thumping.

Parents, the drivers sighed again, would be a whole lot easier to haul.

The counselors, who ranged in age from eighteen to twenty-three, were a bit more subdued than the campers, though somewhat frazzled by the organization process. They waved, held up their hands, counted, greeted, maneuvered the small fry more or less into position around the appropriate signs.

But one man stood out from all the others, and that was Jack "Steamboat" Scarborough, the camp director. He was fifty years old, stood five feet eleven, and weighed 220. He had grizzled, curly short hair, a barrel chest, and short, strong arms as one might expect on a blacksmith. He was not a blacksmith, however, but was, aside from camp director, primarily a high school football coach. His teams lost most of their games, but his players loved him. It was like that with the camp; his Camp Smilin' Through suffered quite a bit in competition with newer, larger ones, but the campers, by and large, loved him.

And one woman, too, stood out from the others. That was Annie "Tugboat" Scarborough, his wife, who supervised the girls' half of the camp. She resembled him physically, an evolution some people thought attributable to the fact that they had been married for thirty years, ever since college. She had short curly hair and strong arms and a square body. She was not, for all that, unattractive. She had the infectious appeal typical of happy, energetic people. Like her husband, she was tough and gentle and hearty and dedicated, and had a crinkly, blue-eyed smile that would melt a polar cap.

A clear difference between them was that those who didn't call him "Mr. Scarborough" called him "Steamboat," while those who didn't call her "Mrs. Scarborough" did not, to her face, call her "Tugboat."

"One boat is plenty in any family," she would say, "and I'm not it."

These two patiently herded the campers into place, treading a careful line between harshness that would worry some of the more protective parents and enough firmness to get the show on the road.

"Come on, everybody!" Steamboat yelled to campers and counselors alike. "Let's get on the doggone buses! They're not gonna wait all day!"

A few of the children stepped into line behind their signs; others thumbed their noses and blew raspberries at the bus drivers. Steamboat spread his arms, moving the boys around; Annie did the same with the girls.

A set of parents walked briskly from their car, pushing their two children in front of them. "Howdy, Steamboat," said the father, "here are ours, ready or not." He smiled and pumped Steamboat's hand.

"Good to see you, Mr. and Mrs. Hinchman," Steamboat said, nodding to them. "Hey there, Wolfman." He put his arm around the stocky, glowering eleven-year-old boy. "Good to see you again." He tossled Michael "Wolfman" Hinchman's curly hair and aimed him at one of the signs. "You're with Harry Driscoll this year, in the Choctaw cabin. Now get going. Nice to have you back, Michelle," he said, turning to Wolfman's sister, who was ten and a near carbon copy of her brother—chunky, with a stubby neck and mousy-gray curly hair. "Gonna have a great summer."

"They always rave about it," Mrs. Hinchman said, nodding brightly. "Always a great summer."

"Well, we try," Steamboat said, watching the brother and sister tacitly head toward their groups. "See you in three weeks."

The experienced campers quickly asserted themselves, meeting their old friends and promising devilment. The new campers cowered silently.

A group of boys stood around the Sioux sign, looking at where the name of Billy Brunkhorst had been crossed out and "The Hulk" crudely printed in black crayon.

"All *right,*" said Bobby Stenzel, a handsome, strong thirteen-year-old blond who was approving of the lettering. "Hey, Hulk, we're gonna knock 'em dead this year!"

"Yeah." Billy Brunkhorst, "The Hulk," was aptly nicknamed. One of the more capable counselors, Hulk was a twenty-year-old who had been extra large since childhood and now weighed in at 240 pounds on a six-four frame. Hulk had been his moniker for as long as he could remember. "In real life," as he put it, he was a third-year psychology student at Bates College in Maine. But during the summer vacation he performed as the consummate camper who knew everything there was to know about camping and animals and wilderness survival—and keeping order in his cabin.

On this last count a certain mythology had developed around Hulk Brunkhorst. It was said that underneath his cheery and pleasant exterior there beat a terrible temper, that Hulk was responsible for the dent in the door of cabin four. In creating the dent, the story went, he had used the head of a particularly nasty twelve-year-old camper as a battering ram. And further, he was said to have invented and perhaps even patented the famed "swirly" on that same occasion. Supposedly he stuck the kid's battered head into the toilet bowl and pulled the chain, at once cleansing and cooling the poor boy's brain.

The legend aside, nobody had ever seen Hulk mistreat anybody, or even lose his temper. And even without the legend, his size and strength alone were enough to command respect and obedience.

Hulk was one of the few people Bobby Stenzel liked and respected. Stenzel, who considered himself, not without grounds, the king of the campers, was big, well developed, and fearless, with the breezy and confident style of the superior athlete he was. Whereas Hulk's reputation was built largely on rumor, Stenzel did in fact employ a quick punch to the nose on occasion to settle a challenge or dispute.

"Who we got this year, Hulk?"

Hulk scanned the list. "Sterling Settlemire, Charlie Stritzinger, and Gale Pincu."

Stenzel wrinkled up his nose. "Hey, man, where's Smitty and Rock the Jock?"

"Didn't come back this year."

"Hey, guys," Bobby yelled to some of the older campers, "we gotta go without Smitty and Rock. Can we do it?"

"Yeah, yeah!" came the replies.

"All *right!*" Bobby jabbed a fist in the air and snapped his head around, causing his long blond hair to swirl.

Off to the side of the parking lot, Annie Scarborough knelt beside two small boys whose mothers clucked over them in vain attempts to stop their crying. To be sure, Annie's first responsibility was to the girl campers. But she extended her motherly umbrella to cover all those problems of homesickness and fear that occurred anywhere among any of the campers—those with problems with which Steamboat could not or would not cope.

"There, there," the mothers said to their boys, "there, there."

And the waves of crying crested anew with each succeeding "there," until Annie discreetly motioned the parents away.

"Okay now, boys," she then said to the two reluctant new campers, "that's enough. Calm down."

A handsome, bearded young man knelt with them. He was Vance Brehm, the most popular counselor.

"Hey, guys, take a break." He smiled at them and they did, in fact, take a break to look at him. "That's better."

Vance always had a way of making things better, at least for everybody else. For himself, he was kind of aimless, or at least uncommitted. Had he been more ambitious, he, rather than Hulk, would have been head counselor. At twenty-three, he was close to becoming a professional student. After scholarly tries at journalism, civil engineering, and archaeology, he was now a student at his fourth college, the University of Southern California (not far from this very parking lot), where he was enrolled in a pre-med course.

Though he wandered a lot in other areas of his life, it was to this camp he always returned, as if it were his rock. Within the camp he was dedicated and directed. A compactly built man with a fetching, dimpled smile, he was a good athlete, a charismatic leader who got his following by encouragement and example rather than dictation. He was a fine storyteller, great around the campfire. He seemed to have a precise sense of timing and of needs of the kids. The camp was nearly a home for him; he had been coming to Camp Smilin' Through since he was eight, and had been a counselor since he was fifteen.

"Now listen, you guys, you're gonna have a real funny counselor. His name is Piano Legs Scarborough." Instantly Vance blushed and glanced at the ground. "Sorry, Mrs. Scarborough. I didn't mean to call him Piano Legs in front of you."

Annie shrugged. The nickname applied to her son was no secret to her—no more than her own. She put her hands on the two boys' shoulders. "What's your name?" she said to the one on her left.

He mumbled something that sounded like "First Star."

"What is it?"

"Furth Sklar," he said more clearly.

"Good. And what's yours?" she asked the other one.

"Clark Kent."

"Heeey!" Vance said, "this boy can rip off his shirt and turn into Supercamper!"

Clark Kent resumed crying.

Vance sighed.

"Okay," Annie said more firmly, turning the boys in the direction of the lines of campers, "time to join up. Furth, you're in Navajo, with Curtis Kirk. Clark, you're an Iroquois, with, um, Chet Scarborough."

"No," Clark Kent said. "I go with Furth. We're both nine and we go together. Else I can't stop crying."

She thought for a second. "Okay. Go ahead." They ran off. "For now," she added. She was pleased to see, across the way, that Steamboat had his arm around their big-legged son, Chet, otherwise known by campers and counselors as Piano Legs. She was pleased to see that, because she thought perhaps there was too little of it, so occupied was Steamboat with a football team one part of the year and a camp another.

"Chet," Steamboat was saying, "I'm expecting real grown-up, responsible behavior from you this year."

"Sure." Piano Legs had a sullen look, but his face was averted from his father.

"We've got a lot of problems and I need your help."

"Yes, dad."

"None of that stuff that went on last year."

"No, daddy." There was an edge to his voice, and the use of the diminutive heightened it—had Steamboat been listening more closely.

"Being a counselor is a sacred trust."

"Absolutely."

"Those little boys look up to you almost like a father."

"Yes, father."

Steamboat's eyes roamed the field of assembling campers, and he smiled and gave Chet's shoulders a final squeeze. "Okay, my fine young bucko, go get 'em!"

Piano Legs winced at the term "bucko," which his father never applied to anybody else. "Okay, dad."

Annie walked up, and Steamboat turned to her while their son ambled off toward the Iroquois sign.

Piano Legs was eighteen, with a small head, thin neck, thin, sloping shoulders, wide hips, enormous thighs and calves and feet. He was like an upside-down version of his father, constructed on the order of a pyramid, so that even eye-to-eye with him one saw him in a kind of diminishing perspective, as if looking up at him from ground level.

Quite naturally he played football. Built as he was —five eight and 190 pounds, with most of his weight below the belt—he had little upper-body strength for tackling, and less speed for running. He was built for being planted on the ground. And so he had played center for three years for his father, the coach. That is to say, he had been a center for three years, but had played little in games. He was not the starter, not even often the backup. Though there were no such fixed assignments as second and third string on Steamboat's teams (everybody not starting being called "ready reserves"), Piano Legs considered himself, resentfully, third string.

His resentment derived not alone from the fact that he was third string, but from the fact that since the team had lost eight of its nine games the past season, there was every reason to shake up the lineup and get him in there. After all, he felt, he could snap the ball into the quarterback's hands as crisply as the other centers, and he was not all *that* bad a blocker.

All in all, Piano Legs felt that he was relegated to third string because his father refused to see him as a football player like the others and perceived him only as his little boy. Summer camp was where Piano Legs took out his frustrations.

Piano Legs arrived at his sign and looked over the line of small boys. With some satisfaction he spied the familiar face of Alan Friedman, a tiny ten-year-old.

Alan was in the familiar act of spilling his gear all over the place. He was scrambling around on hands and knees recovering items that had tumbled out of his duffel bag. Every time he stuffed something in, something else fell out.

Piano Legs bent down beside him. "Here, I'll give you a hand."

"I don't know why this always happens to me," Alan said.

Piano Legs helped him repack all his gear; then, looking around to make sure nobody was watching, he reached down and grabbed the back of Alan's pants, pulled up, and twisted hard.

"Ow! Ow!" Alan winced painfully from the first "snuggy" of the new camp season.

"If you mess up this summer, you little nerd," Piano Legs said, his lip curling meanly, "you're getting a snuggy in the morning and a swirly at night, understand?"

Alan nodded quickly. It was not an auspicious beginning to the new camp session, but it was not, for him, unusual. It would not be his last snuggy. Alan, who had always been small, had learned, like some of the other small ones, to hang in.

Things were beginning to get organized. There came running up a boy and girl of unusual thinness.

"Paper Man!" somebody called out. The boy, Raymond Smith, waved shyly.

His sister, Rosemary, slapped his shoulder. "I thought you said nobody'd call you that this year," she hissed.

"Just be happy nobody calls *you* that, skinny," he said.

"Hey, Paper Woman!" called one of the girls.

She blushed deeply and ignored the slap on the shoulder from her brother. She scowled over at the Cherokee line from which had come the unwelcome greeting.

The two had been coming to the camp for three

years, and the "Paper" names had been hung on them since the first. With each new session they both hoped to see some signs of their stick-bodies filling out. So far, just all tall bones.

Over at the Seminole sign stood a lean and stringy young woman named Gerri Belardi, the counselor. Given to such lonely athletic pursuits as long-distance running, she wore a "Boston Marathon" T-shirt. She looked around nervously. "Where's Robin Holt?" she asked one of the three girls there. None answered.

One of the three was June Grabowsky, a bony-faced, ungainly, and withdrawn girl of thirteen who yearned for acceptance by the other two, Dee Dee Keough and Dianne Wingo.

But such acceptance was nowhere near. Dee Dee and Dianne were the camp sirens—Dee Dee the more obviously developed and obvious flirt. Dee Dee, who had long blond hair and bedroom eyes, was known to smoke cigarettes. She was Dianne's model.

Dianne had shorter, swept-back dark hair, and her eyes were more innocent.

A boy strutted past and poked Dianne in the ribs. "Your feet stink," he said.

She poked him back. "Get stuffed." Dianne was not as flashy as Dee Dee, nor did she have the bravado and flair. Nor would her parents allow her to smoke. "You're lucky not to have a brother, Dee Dee."

Though the two thirteen-year-olds were both secretly admired by the younger girls for their relative poise and good looks, Dianne did feel that her having a brother—the one who had just poked her—held her back. Dee Dee, in her view, had an advantage in not having to suffer the indignities inflicted by brothers.

"Even if I did," said Dee Dee, jutting out a hip, "I wouldn't take that crap."

"What am I supposed to do? Even though Turkey's only twelve," she said, using her brother Hal's nickname, "he's as big as I am." She assumed a pose just like Dee Dee's.

"You gotta learn to handle men," Dee Dee said coolly. "You smoking yet, by the way?"

"When I feel like it."

"I been smoking since I was twelve," Dee Dee said proudly. "Two packs a day now."

June Grabowsky took a cautious step toward her. "Gee, you smoke?"

"Who asked you?" Dee Dee said.

June retreated.

Dee Dee caught Bobby Stenzel's eye and gave him a come-hither smile, pursing her lips.

Keeping his eye on her, he strutted away, unfortunately walking into the fender of a car.

Dee Dee laughed.

"Boy, what a skaggy bunch of males," Dianne said, turning up her nose.

"Bobby Stenzel's cute," Dee Dee said.

"He's okay."

"He's mine any time I want him."

"Probably *anybody*'s."

"Don't kid yourself."

Robin Holt, a slender, bright-eyed girl as vivacious as a colt, finally arrived with her parents. She stopped to give them each a good-bye kiss. Her mother looked approvingly at Dee Dee and Dianne, who were nearby and watching.

"Those your cabin mates, Robin?" her mother asked. "They look like very nice girls."

Robin rolled her eyes. "Sure, mom." She waved to Gerri Belardi, her counselor, who waved back, looking relieved.

Gerri *was* relieved to see Robin arrive. Gerri was a good camp instructor whose primary interest was in sports. Dee Dee and Dianne, with their vamping and flirting, were not her cup of tea. Robin, though rather shy and interested in no sport but canoeing, was pleasant and cooperative and more to Gerri's liking.

At the Sioux lineup. Hulk Brunkhorst greeted his last boy, Charlie Stritzinger. Bobby Stenzel gave Charlie a perfunctory nod without speaking.

"Well, Charlie," Hulk said enthusiastically, "it's you and Bobby and Gale Pincu and old Sterling Settlemire and me against the world."

Charlie smiled wanly.

"Hey," Hulk said more confidentially, "it could be worse. Rock the Jock went to YMCA camp. Smitty dropped out altogether. Thank goodness for small favors, hunh?"

Charlie nodded, a bit relieved, and waved cheerily to Sterling, who waved back.

Gale Pincu, a round and good-natured and often-teased boy, shuffled over to say hi to Charlie, one of the few campers who did not put him down for his girth or clumsiness or lack of athletic skills.

Bobby Stenzel goosed Gale. "Hey, Pincu, is that your face or did your pants fall down?"

Some of the nearby boys from the Choctaw and Mohawk cabins laughed, giving Bobby encouragement.

Gale just shuffled past, mumbling something.

"Don't let it bother you," Charlie said. "How ya doin'?"

Charlie was a witty and pleasant boy, but rather an introvert who liked to spend his time reading. Camp was not really his bag, but he accepted it as his duty and made the best of it. Neither athlete nor fighter—not competitive in any obvious way—he strove to avoid sports and stay out of Bobby Stenzel's way. He was not disliked, but didn't pal around much with anybody. He was fond of Hulk, his counselor, and was crazy about Steamboat. He was not particularly fond of the lumbering Gale Pincu, but was not one to tread upon the downtrodden.

"I'm doing okay," Gale said, "now that you're here."

"Aw . . ."

Only three little girls were present at the Cheyenne sign, which was just fine with the counselor, Kiki Watwood. Kiki, twenty-two, had hated camp as a child and didn't like it much better as a counselor She had a degree in hotel management, but had not been able to find a job. Camp counselor was better than nothing.

One of her girls, Debbie Settlemire, Sterling's little sister, stood quietly sucking her thumb.

Another, Marian Pincu, Gale's little sister, stood with her doting parents who baby-talked to her. "Gonna have a nice time in the sweet camp-ums, darlin'?" cooed her mother.

"My little punkin gonna be a good girl?" asked her father.

"We'll send you brownies every day."

Marian basked in the attention of her parents.

The third little girl was Barbie Lipski, who, still holding her mother's hand, raved to Kiki about her previous summer. "It was at this wonderful camp in the Catskills, you know, upstate New York? Marvie kids and food and motorboats and indoor tennis courts and Olympic swimming pool and horses and just *everything*."

Kiki nodded, waited until Barbie's parents had left, then said to her, "Hey, Barbie? Who cares about your rich kids' camp?"

Annie Scarborough blew a whistle and the kids started loading onto the buses. Parents waved from their cars. Counselors prodded their charges forward. There were tears and smiles and cheers.

Steamboat approached Annie anxiously. "The Gladstones still aren't here."

"Oh no?"

"Nope. We're supposed to have thirty-seven kids. We only got thirty-three. Thirty-seven is bad enough, for cryin' out loud. We can hardly afford to lose anybody. Where the devil are the Gladstones?"

"Beats me."

"Annie, why don't you go in some place and call them. Tell them to get down here or they're gonna be left behind."

"Okay."

"Wait. If they don't like that, tell them—tell them I'll carry those four kids up there on my back."

"Right." She smiled and started away. Then she stopped short, pointing. "Hey, here comes Mrs. Gladstone!"

Mrs. Gladstone, chicly dressed in a camel hair suit and brilliantly coifed, walked toward them, alone.

"Hey," Steamboat called, trying to conceal his concern, "where are your kids?"

She stood sheepishly before Steamboat and Annie. "Well, um, the fact is, unh, I'm not sending my children with you this year. I know I should have called—"

"What?" Steamboat slapped his forehead. "They've been coming out with us for three years! Why all of a sudden?"

"Well, um, the Parkers and the Lufburrows took their children out, and—"

"I know that, but—"

"Well, they're neighbors of ours, and, um, well, we all finally decided to send our kids to the YMCA camp."

"The Y camp?" Steamboat looked very pained.

"It's bigger and has better facilities," she said defensively. "You've got to admit that yourself, Mr. Scarborough."

"Well, sure, they have more organized activities and more comfortable cabins, but there are certain intangibles at Smilin' Through. Gee, we kind of counted on you."

"I'm really sorry, Mr. Scarborough. Thanks for everything over the years." She turned abruptly and went away.

Steamboat and Annie were stunned. They were used to setbacks, but things were getting critical.

"No Early Birds at all this year," Steamboat moaned, "and only thirty-three kids."

"Well, that's the way it is," Annie said, squaring her jaw. "We'll live with it."

"Yeah." He turned toward the buses and waved. "Let's move out!" he yelled. "Let 'em roll!"

He and Annie jumped aboard separate buses, and out they rolled.

CHAPTER
2

The buses wheeled out of the parking lot and onto the freeway, headed for the hills northeast of Los Angeles where was located Camp Smilin' Through.

On the boys' bus, Bobby Stenzel dominated as usual. He told bad jokes, but every one got the dutiful laugh. Not to laugh at Stenzel's jokes was to risk alienation from the king, and maybe a snuggy or two later. And anyway, Stenzel was fun to be around. He was action.

Even Hulk, sitting next to him in front, laughed at his jokes—though not to ingratiate himself, but because he always laughed at the kids' jokes.

"Hear the latest about Gale Pincu?" Bobby called back through the bus. "He must be jelly 'cause jam don't shake like that!"

Belches of laughter greeted him. Gale slunk down in his seat.

One seat from the rear, Curtis Kirk, counselor of the Navajo cabin, sat with a very small boy named Harvey Allen. Harvey, a first-time camper at eight years of age, was very bright and in love with handicrafts. Going to camp was the greatest adventure of his life. And he was sitting with just the right guy.

Curtis Kirk, at eighteen a young counselor, was a willowy, pale, scholarly man whose specialties were drama, crafts, and Indian lore. Personally, he was not a favorite of the other counselors or of Steamboat. He was a bit prissy for their tastes. But on the other hand, he was tolerated gladly for his talent at putting on shows, whipping up sets and costumes out of virtually nothing (virtually nothing was all the budget allowed), and telling Indian tales. He loved getting into costume and war paint, although he looked absurd with his sallow skin and scrawny arms and thick glasses.

Curtis captivated many of the younger campers with his enthusiasm. And the enthusiasm was real; he would study Indian culture at Sarah Lawrence College in the fall.

"You gonna tell us about Indians?" Harvey asked.

"You bet. And we're gonna dress up in true Indian style and be creatures of the woods."

"Boy!"

"Grooovy!" called Turkey Wingo sarcastically, looking up the aisle for approval from Bobby Stenzel. Hal "Turkey" Wingo, Dianne's younger brother, also had a brother in camp, ten-year-old Preston. But he was like neither of them. Turkey as he came to be known for the time he found a wild chicken in the woods and came racing into camp proclaiming it to be a turkey—was a chunky, loud, well-liked boy who loved rough-and-tumble sports. Though slow afoot, he was agile and strong, one of the best athletes in camp. Aside from the times he played up to Bobby, he was really a friendly and compassionate sort.

Unfortunately, like many in the camp, his friendliness was often obscured by the desire to catch the eyes of the kings and queens. His sister Dianne, one of the queens, was anything but a queen to him. But Dee Dee on the other hand—who could ignore her considerable charms? And the only way to be anywhere near Dee Dee was to be a friend of Bobby Stenzel.

Sitting across the aisle from Curtis Kirk were the two new little boys who had been crying earlier—Clark Kent and Furth Sklar. They were still sniffling.

"Hey, friends," Curtis said in his cheery manner, "want me to tell you a story?"

They shook their heads.

He turned to Harvey. "Tell me, Harvey, what do you like more than anything else in the world?"

"Cats."

"Oh, that's beautiful. Let's sing a little song, to cheer everybody up." He leaned across the aisle. "Boys, a little song?" They shook their heads again, but he ignored that. "Do you know *The Farmer in the Dell*?"

"Do you know the farmer's daughter?" came the rude reply from the backmost seat.

Curtis spun around to see Piano Legs slouched beside another counselor, Harry Driscoll, both smirking.

"Oooh, that's just beautiful!" Harry cooed.

"Leave me alone!" Curtis snapped. "You aren't even sitting with your boys like you're supposed to."

"Let 'em be," Harry said. "We'll see enough of the little monsters in the next month."

Harry Driscoll, tall, dark, and sly, was not one of life's achievers. He was plenty bright enough, and perceptive, but lazy—or, as psychologists might have it, unmotivated. He drifted through his existence taking whatever was offered and giving very little in return. He was witty enough, and made few demands on anybody, and was therefore liked to a reasonable degree by the other counselors.

To the kids he was anathema, much like Piano Legs Scarborough, his partner in deviltry. He had a cruel streak in him, more a product of an idle, bored mind than of sadism. He wasn't all that fond of Piano Legs, in point of fact, because Piano Legs wasn't as bright and clever. But he, alone among the counselors, would share Piano Legs's bag of dirty tricks. He was almost as good as Piano Legs at giving snuggies.

"Besides," Harry went on, elbowing Piano Legs in the ribs, "the monsters will see enough of *us* too, guaranteed."

He and Piano Legs slid further down in their seat, and Harry lit up a cigarette.

"Hey, my dad might see you," Piano Legs whispered nervously.

"So? What's he gonna do, kick me out of camp? He's got barely enough of us as it is."

In the seat ahead, Curtis, sniffing smoke, turned around. "I'll tell."

"You do," Harry said calmly, "and I'll break your whimpy little wrists."

"Hmmph!" Curtis flounced back around forward in his seat, his arms folded across his chest.

Now his seat mate, Harvey Allen, got up on his knees and faced over the back of the seat, as innocently curious about the smoking as he was about every aspect of the camp.

Harry blew smoke in his face. "Beat it."

Harvey slipped quickly down into his seat.

Up front, a happy eleven-year-old loudly issued challenges. "I'll take anybody one-on-one in basketball, or any kind of skateboarding!"

There were some raspberries, but not too much of a razz. Clark Brunkhorst, The Hulk's younger brother, was a skateboard ace. He was husky and tough like his brother and tried to imitate him in every way. His hero, outside of Hulk, was Jack Lambert, the hard-hitting linebacker of the Pittsburgh Steelers. He only wished he had a picture of Lambert on a skateboard. He was already on his way to being a fine athlete. For all his braggadocio posing, he was, like his brother, well liked.

"Come on, anybody, put up or shut up! I got the winner at anything!"

"You got the size, too," said Vance Brehm, his popular counselor and himself a good athlete. Vance scratched his beard. "We're gonna have to call you the Mini-Hulk this year."

Clark beamed with pleasure. So did Hulk, sitting across the aisle.

"Hulk," Vance said, "we're gonna have some real good times this year, you know that?"

"You're right. Gonna be some good, tough competition."

Several of the boys left their seats to gather around Vance.

"What new goodies you got lined up for this year, Vance?" asked Turkey Wingo.

"Yeah, we gonna have belching contests this year again?" asked Wolfman Hinchman. Wolfman was not a great belcher. What he was known as was a head-butter. He was called Wolfman because he had a large head and eyebrows that grew together just under his hairline, giving him a perpetually fierce look. When he got into a fight, his technique was to butt his opponent in the stomach or the head or wherever there was an opening. And nobody had a head as hard as Wolfman's.

"Belching is no longer cool," said Thornton Stanfield.

" 'Cause you can't," Turkey said.

"We ought to be more dignified by now," Thornton said. Thornton Stanfield was dignified already at eleven. He was very bright, a bookworm, had skipped a grade in school. He was well spoken, neat, polite, and considerate. He was also the only black boy in camp, as his sister, Hazel, was the only black girl.

Thornton was not proud of being black, nor was he ashamed of it. To himself, he barely acknowledged the fact. "I am not a stereotype," he would say to anyone who asked him about civil rights or black consciousness or sports.

"Anyone can belch," Thornton said.

"Aw, do one, Vance!" Clark Brunkhorst pleaded.

"Yeah, yeah."

"Okay," Vance said, "just one."

He loosed a seven-second rolling, bubbling belch that brought a cheer from his surrounding admirers. Several of them started belching.

"Okay, knock it off," Vance said. They did. "We're gonna think of something new this year."

"Something really great?" Wolfman asked.

"Yup."

"Well, if it's not belching, maybe we could have raids on the girls' side, and pull—"

"No."

"But something really really great?" Wolfman persisted.

"Yup. Maybe a new kind of crazy dive."

"Wowee!" Wolfman jumped straight up and rammed his head into the ceiling of the bus, making a noticeable dent and bringing a "Whoop!" from his fans.

Charlie Stritzinger, sitting nearby with Sterling Settlemire, winced. "Gonna be a long summer," he mumbled.

Steamboat, sitting right behind the driver, stared straight ahead up the road, thinking and worrying.

The girls' bus was, of course, much quieter. The same forces and byplay and expectations were at work, the same assertion of position and jockeying for prestige, but it was all more subdued, deceptively calm.

Dee Dee and Dianne slouched together across the aisle from Robin and June.

"Age doesn't seem to have *matured* you any," Dee Dee said to Robin, looking her up and down.

Robin shrugged. "I don't care."

"Neither do any *boys* that I know of," Dee Dee said, chortling.

"I'm beginning to, um, fill out," June Grabowsky put in hopefully.

"Who cares?" Dee Dee said.

"That's nice, June," Robin said, laughing lightly and patting her on the arm. "That's really terrific."

Though Robin's ostensibly comforting words might have been taken by some as mild sarcasm, June smiled gratefully. Any compliments, however borderline, were welcome, especially around Dee Dee and Dianne, who, when not making patronizing comments, seemed altogether bored with her. Anyway, Robin was seldom sarcastic.

Counselor Gerri Belardi turned around and looked over her seatback at Robin. "I'm really glad to have you in our cabin," she said confidentially, "since all these other creeps are only interested in boys."

"Thanks."

"You know, Robin, you could be great at track. I've been noticing your calf muscles and your latissimus dorsi—good and long, perfect for developing as a runner."

"What are latissiness doorseye?"

"Back muscles, lower back. Yours are long and firm and tapered, like mine. You have the build of a runner."

"How come you know all about that?"

"I major in kinesiology at UCLA—the study of body movement and anatomy. I can identify every muscle in the body."

"That sounds very healthy."

"It *is*, believe me. Much more healthy than thinking about boys all the time, like some people I could mention." She shot a glance over at Dee Dee and Dianne, who were staring, bored, out the window. "You want to work on it, on developing those muscles for running? I'm getting in shape for the Boston Marathon. Twenty-six miles. Very few women have done it."

"Sure, Gerri. I'll give it some serious thought. But I don't think I could ever run twenty-six miles."

"Sure you could. We'll do it a little at a time."

"Well, I'll sure think about it."

Toward the back sat the girl who looked a lot like Wolfman—his sister, Michelle. Wolfman looked a little meaner than she did. Her eyebrows were not quite so heavy and did not collide in so large a bundle of fur at the center of her forehead. But it was Michelle who *was* meaner.

Next to her sat a very clean and prim girl named

Joyce Cuccinello. Joyce was holding a doll dressed in Quaker clothes. She smoothed the doll's blond hair.

"Can I see it?" Michelle asked nicely.

"Um, well, okay." She handed it over.

"Very nice," Michelle said, turning it around and nodding. Then, with a grunt, she leaned down and bit off a hunk of the doll's hair, leaving a bald spot.

"No!" Joyce, in tears, snatched the doll back and hugged it tight. "See what you did!"

"Just thought I'd save you the trouble of combing her—"

A *whack,* more loud than hard, came across the back of Michelle's head from her counselor, B.J. Littlefield.

Michelle slumped down in her seat, smiling.

"It's okay," B.J. said, tapping the top of Joyce's head. "Actually the doll doesn't look bad with a bald spot. Kind of individual."

B.J.—Brenda Jane, a name she had abandoned as soon as she could—was rather individual herself. A large and friendly woman of nineteen, she was one of the more respected leaders. She was a terrific athlete. Back east, where she grew up in a suburb of New York, she was a terror at field hockey and lacrosse. In her freshman year at UCLA, she led the girls' basketball team in scoring and rebounding. She had been a camper from her earliest days, and a counselor for four years. Though she was liked by all the counselors, she gravitated toward the males, with whom she could enjoy the wrestling and arm-pounding and horseplay she favored. One of her most endearing performances among the campers, however, occurred when she adopted the voice of Howard Cosell to narrate activities from the sidelines.

Unlike Gerri Belardi, B.J. was interested in boys. Nothing obvious, but in fact she had a light crush on Hulk. Perhaps he had a crush on her too, but that was something Hulk himself wasn't fully aware of. Their relationship consisted of sitting together often and punching each other in the shoulders. On more serious occasions, they would arm-wrestle. The clue to their relationship was that however strong B.J. was for a woman, Hulk could easily have thrown down her arm. Instead, their bouts lasted several minutes, more like vigorous hand-holding.

B.J. was aware of the camp's deficiencies, but doted on Steamboat and Annie. The two directors were, in her eyes, the sort of kind and caring and energetic people who ought to run society.

"Aw, come on, Joyce," she went on, "stop crying now. We're gonna go camping and play baseball and all that nifty stuff. What's so important about dolls, anyway?"

"They're *beautiful*." Joyce clutched her doll more tightly.

"Oh, sure, but getting out and actually *doing* things is more fun. That's more important than dolls, don't you think?"

"No."

"Why not?"

"That's my own business," Joyce said tearfully, pushing herself back into the corner with her doll.

Gerri wandered back to talk to counselor Stacy Brunkhorst, older sister of Clark and younger one of Hulk.

"I'm going to run in the Boston Marathon," Gerri said proudly.

"Really? That's terrif!" There was no sarcasm in her voice or in her heart. Outside of the fact that she was the sister of Hulk and Clark, there was no apparent family resemblance. Stacy was a petite five foot one, with short curly black hair. The most common adjective applied to her was "cute." The next most common was "nice."

Older girls tended to be envious of her face and figure; little girls tended to get crushes on her and follow her around. She was fiercely determined never to smoke or drink, talk dirty, or knowingly play up to boys. Not that she wasn't interested in boys. One inhibition in that regard came from the fact that her protective older brother might destroy any boy laying a hand on her.

Stacy, whose aim was to be an elementary school teacher, was in charge of the youngest girls in camp. And she loved them.

"Been training for eight months," Gerri went on. "I try to run five miles a day now. I'll get it up to ten a day soon. Then the marathon."

"Will you be running with just women," piped up another counselor, Jane Smith, "or with men?"

"The men," Gerri said firmly.

"Right on!" Jane raised a fist. "Up with women!"

Jane Smith was a study in contrasts. She admired the independence and dedication of Gerri Belardi—not at all put off by the fact that Gerri had long dishwater-colored hair, large ears that stuck straight out, and rather horsey features. She admired Gerri's well-toned muscles, which some other people thought were gross and unfeminine. Yet Jane herself, without trying or even thinking about it, was even cuter than Stacy Brunkhorst, with soft and subtle curves and long, dark, shining hair.

Jane was a cheerful and capable camper who enjoyed all activities, but her major interest lay in the work of such organizations as Women Against Violence to Women, the National Organization for Women, and those pushing the Equal Rights Amendment. From time to time at camp she would rail that girls were treated like second-class citizens. Rape, to her, was the most serious of all crimes, and often she lectured the small girls about the dangers of rape and the ways to protect themselves against it—oblivious to the fact that the little girls didn't have the foggiest notion of what she was talking about.

Nor did anyone else, really, for her own grasp of the issues was unclear. But they were issues—they were *her* issues. She was determined not to go through life being just another pretty face. Nobody was offended by her aggressive—if only verbal—feminism. She was not a hostile woman.

The three counselors huddled together.

"Boy, I think it's terrible that there are so few campers this year," Gerri said. "Wonder if they'll be cutting back on the overnight camp-outs."

"I doubt it," Jane said, "especially not so long as *you're* there to run them so well."

"I have a feeling the camp's not gonna last after this year," Stacy said. "Not since old man Bolin died. I'm really gonna miss it."

"Well, if Bolin's son is as good a man as his father was, he'll keep the camp running, no matter what," Jane said. "And if he doesn't, we'll organize all the girls and march on him."

"Does anybody know if he'll be the same kind of owner as his father was?" Gerri asked.

"Why shouldn't he be?"

"I don't know anything about him," Stacy said, "except that I think he used to be a camper."

"Well, that's something," Jane said. "He must have some loyalties."

"But with so few campers . . ."

"Why don't we just look on the bright side?"

A little black-haired girl with Oriental features, Cathy Shimizu, came shyly up to them. "Stacy, can I sit with you?"

"Sure, Cathy, good to see you."

"I'm so glad you're my counselor," Cathy said, leaning against Stacy.

"So'm I," Stacy said resignedly, ignoring the smiles exchanged between Jane and Gerri.

Jane turned her attention to two new sniffling ten-year-olds who were going to be in her Penobscot cabin. "Homesick?"

The girls nodded together.

"Now you listen to me. We're going to have fun, okay?"

The girls nodded, still sniffling.

"And listen, stop crying. Boys don't cry, right? So I don't want to see any girls crying because girls are as strong as boys—*stronger*." She fixed them with a firm gaze. "You got that?"

They stopped crying.

"Good. That's showing me some moxie."

Behind them, Hazel Stanfield, Thornton's sister, was playing a card game of Go Fish with Rosemary Smith.

"You can't beat me, Paper Woman. You been trying to beat me for three years. Nobody can beat me. I'm the smartest girl in camp and the best Go Fish player."

"Stop it," Paper Woman said testily. "You got any threes?"

"Go fish!" Hazel thrust her face forward and stuck out her tongue.

"Got it!" She held up the three she had just drawn. "So?"

"Got any jacks?"

"Go fish."

She drew a seven.

"Got any sevens?" Hazel asked.

"Geez, I just drew it!"

"Nobody can beat me," Hazel said, plucking the seven out of her hand. "Gonna be like this all summer!"

Leaning back in her seat, Dianne asked Dee Dee, "You going after Bobby Stenzel this summer?"

"I might," Dee Dee said coolly. "I just might. He's the only boy worth going after in the whole camp."

"If you ask me, he's a little young."

"For who?" Dee Dee eyed her.

"For me. I'm going after Vance Brehm."

"Vance?" She scoffed. "You're crazy. Since when do you think you can get a counselor, especially Vance? He's probably got a string of girls back home—girls *his* age."

"So?"

"So if you get Vance, I'm Farrah Fawcett-Majors."

"You just wait." Dianne pouted a little. "And you better start letting your hair grow."

"You're full of beans. If Vance was free, he'd probably let *me* know about it."

"Oh? How?"

"Some sign, you know. They let you know when they're available."

"Well, you just wait for your silly *sign*. I'm going after him."

"You can call me Farrah."

From time to time Annie turned around from her front seat to survey the load of girls. She smiled at them, enjoying the snippets of their conversation and songs and games. But she was worried. At least as worried as Steamboat. They both had loved old Mr. Bolin. Steamboat thought his son, Freddy, would be just fine. But she wasn't so sure. There was something about his eyes.

The buses wound up the mountain roads, leaving civilization behind and becoming surrounded by towering pines. For some of the new campers, it was an exciting scene, and they looked expectantly for deer and bears and all the wild animals they had heard about.

"Same old trees," Dee Dee said.

"Aren't they beautiful?" June Grabowsky offered.

"I'm more into flesh and blood," Dee Dee said naughtily, drawing a chuckle from Dianne.

In the boys' bus, Hulk Brunkhorst eyed the scenery carefully. "Looks like it was a good winter, Steamboat. Everything's thick and heavy. Camp ought to be beautiful."

"Yeah," Steamboat said vacantly. He was trying to maintain optimism in the face of his concerns. Generally he worried just like Annie, about the same things, but he tended to be more optimistic, saw things more rosily, expected the best from people—people like the new owner, Freddy Bolin.

That was where he and Annie were a little different, in how they saw certain situations. Annie felt she was more realistic. Like with Steamboat's teams. Aside from the fact that they lost a lot and that his job might be in some jeopardy because of that, he didn't care all that much about winning. His attitude was that football should be fun and was valuable for getting kids in shape and developing cooperative team spirit.

Annie, on the other hand, while not believing in winning at any cost, still felt that winning was good for people. And she thought Steamboat should have a better record. She thought he could have been a successful college coach, since his technical knowledge of the intricacies of football was superior and went largely to waste at the high school level.

She felt he should be more organized and ambitious—not for prestige or to improve their lifestyle necessarily, but for his own sense of satisfaction. The bottom line, however, was that despite her small pressures on him to change a little, he was the boss and she backed him to the hilt in whatever he did.

She even supported—hard as it was for her—his decision not to play their son at center more. But she worried more than he did about Piano Legs's reaction to riding the bench. She wished father and son were closer, shared themselves more with each other.

Actually, what she wanted was for her son to be as fine a man as his father.

When it came to camp, Annie was indispensable. Steamboat was at a total loss to comprehend special problems and needs of girls. That entire side of it was left to her. And Annie was a gem. She had never had a daughter of her own, and she lavished her love on all these girls as if they were hers.

Steamboat always wished she would worry less about the finances of the camp, leave that all to him. Even though he worried himself, he was sure it would work out somehow. Although four more campers would have helped him balance the books.

But the deeper they drove into the wilderness, the less he worried. The outdoors always buoyed him. It would be a good camp, just like always. At camp, he was the boss—no school principals, faculty meetings, boards of education to look over his shoulder. And when he was in charge of things, they went right. It would be a good camp, just like always.

They turned onto a gravel road and several minutes later pulled into a clearing by a small lake.

And they were at Camp Smilin' Through.

The most commonly uttered expression in the two buses as the campers first caught sight of the camp was "Geez."

CHAPTER
3

Everybody felt let down. The newcomers had been built up to expect something better. The experienced campers expected at least what they remembered. Even Steamboat was a little disappointed.

The setting of the camp, spreading out over fifty acres or so, was indeed pretty and rustic. Tall, thick pines surrounded it, and the afternoon sun glinted off Drum Lake.

But the buildings and immediate grounds, at best decent, were not the manicured, well-tended environs suggested in the camp brochures. Weeds were knee-high throughout the site. The wood of the dining halls, lavatories, and cabins was warped from weather, and the paint was flaking off in big chunks. The aluminum canoes, left last fall on the dining hall roof, had been blown off, apparently in some spring storm, and lay scattered here and there in various positions, right side up, upside down, and sideways, dented and scratched. Door hinges had rusted and sagged on all the buildings. The docks on both the girls' and boys' sides of the lake lay tilted in the water—perhaps the result of the same storm.

Some of the new kids were shocked and put their hands over their mouths. Kids making comments were told to keep still by counselors who made the same comments. For the older kids and counselors, the gist of the remarks was this: the camp was a mess. It looked worse this year than ever before.

It *was* worse. Ushering kids out of the buses, Steamboat muttered, "There wasn't time or money to get anybody out here ahead of time to fix things up like we usually do."

Campers clustered around the buses, reluctant to step forward into their summer homes.

"Come on, come on." Steamboat urged them forward. "I have a surprise for everybody that will guarantee some healthful exercise this first afternoon. After lunch, all boys and girls will gather at the council ring."

The girls and boys separated, Annie leading the girls around to their side of the lake, Steamboat herding the boys toward their cabins.

When Steamboat and Annie had first taken over Camp Smilin' Through eighteen years before, everything had been in terrible shape. Buildings were delapidated, and some had to be entirely replaced. Plumbing to the kitchens and lavatories leaked woefully and had to be replaced. So overgrown was the site with brush and vines and weeds that it took them two full weeks to clear it. But by the second year the camp was quite splendid by comparison.

Some years had passed during which the camp was maintained well. Unfortunately, in later years, as costs of maintenance had increased, the number of campers had decreased. Old Mr. Bolin, from whom Steamboat leased the camp, had poured quite a bit of money into it, but his funds were not unlimited.

And then this winter the old man had died, leaving the camp to his son, Freddy. Obviously Freddy had not been inclined, or had not been able, to spend the money to make necessary repairs for this season. What's more, this was the first year in which there had been no Early Birds at all—those campers who elected to come out early for an extra week.

That is not to say the camp was a disaster area. With some work it would be made habitable and pleasant. Drum Lake, from the bottom of which more and more garbage surfaced each summer so that it was often referred to as "Scum Lake" by cynical campers, was perhaps a hundred yards wide and served to divide the girls' side from the boys'. There was not a total division, for many activities were shared together—council rings, dances, handicraft classes, and other events.

The two sides of the camp were much alike. Both dining halls were rustic buildings fifty feet long with open-hearth fireplaces, kitchens in the back, and picnic tables and benches and huge screened windows. On each side were seven roomy cabins, of which only five on each side would be in use this season. Like the dining halls, they were built up off the ground on concrete pilings and were constructed of weathered redwood. The wooden walls extended halfway up, screens the rest of the way to the eaves. In each cabin were five bunks—actually iron army cots—with accompanying iron lockers. Single bare bulbs provided the light.

All the structures were connected by well-worn paths, and on both sides of the lake the paths converged in a slope leading to the docks that extended into the lake about ten yards. On the boys' side, the slope was steeper, and an asphalt sidewalk had been installed from the dining hall to the dock—a request fulfilled by Steamboat for use as a skateboarding track.

Also on the boys' side was a small, four-room, single-story cottage where Steamboat and Annie lived. Adjacent to it was the parking lot.

Behind the camp buildings on both sides were playing fields for baseball, basketball, and soccer. On the girls' side there was an archery range.

The facilities, while not extensive or fancy, were adequate. Everything had seemed fine indeed until larger camps were developed in the area.

These larger camps were run mostly by large, well-financed organizations such as the YMCA, YMHA, the Episcopal Diocese of Greater Los Angeles, and large corporations and foundations. They were equipped with riding stables, Olympic-size swimming pools, professional dramatic teachers and athletic coaches; they provided uniforms for various activities and served more expensive food.

While there were many miles of woods surrounding Camp Smilin' Through, with places for camping out, trails for hiking, and secret places to hide in, there was really no way for Camp Smilin' Through to compete with the fancier camps—at least in the eyes of the parents who paid the fees. And so it was to these larger, more affluent, modern camps that campers were being lured, leaving, this year, only thirty-three for Smilin' Through.

The bottom line was that Steamboat Scarborough was caught in a downward spiral. The fewer kids he had, the less money he took in, and then the more run-down the camp became. The more run-down the camp became, the fewer kids he could attract. And so on.

Were he a wealthy man, he could continue to operate at a deficit—and would gladly, in fact, because he did this really for the good of his soul and the souls of the kids.

It might have seemed like a losing battle. Camp Smilin' Through had no Early Birds this year and only four new campers. There were ten counselors, several of whom would not have been hired in better times.

By the time the food bills were paid, Steamboat would be nearly broke.

And with the football record he had left behind, and the comments it was causing around the Booster Club, he couldn't even be sure he would have a job to go back to.

Still, for all this, Steamboat had his own bottom line, different from what outsiders might have. His bottom line was that thirty-three kids had come to Camp Smilin' Through this summer, and he would see to it that they all had one heck of a good time.

Older campers sprinted for their cabins, intent on staking out the best spaces for themselves.

Bobby Stenzel was first to reach the Sioux cabin, where the thirteen-year-olds lived. He burst through the door and dove for the best bunk in the far corner, sprawling over it.

"Out!" Hulk, coming in, waggled a thumb. "Out. Counselor's bunk."

"Aw . . ."

Then Bobby, seeing Gale Pincu approach, jumped up and grabbed the next best bunk in the opposite corner.

Gale lumbered, sighing, through the door and started to sit on the closest bunk, only to be elbowed aside by Charlie Stritzinger.

"Mine!" Charlie announced, asserting himself in one of the few chances he would get.

Gale turned and started to sit down on another bunk when Sterling Settlemire beat him to it. Gale had to settle for the worst bunk, worse than the others only because it sagged more in the middle—which any of the bunks would do, in fact, with him on it.

"What're you doing, Stenzel?" Hulk demanded. He knew exactly what Bobby was doing, which was hanging up a centerfold picture from *Playboy* magazine. "Take it down."

"Aw . . ."

"Down."

Bobby took it down, to the accompaniment of giggles from his cabin mates.

In the Mohawk cabin for the twelve-year-olds, Turkey Wingo grabbed the best bunk. Thornton Stanfield was next in. He set his gear carefully on the floor, picked up a rag, and began his usual fastidious dusting of everything.

Raymond Smith, Paper Man, lay down on the floor next to his bunk and commenced doing sit-ups— another of his vain attempts to put some size on himself.

"Don't break yourself in two," said Vance Brehm, his counselor.

In the Choctaw cabin, Wolfman Hinchman and Clark Brunkhorst gaily threw down their duffel bags and grabbed each other in wrestling holds. They banged around the cabin, ramming into the bed of their counselor, Harry Driscoll.

"Snuggies for the next guy that touches my bed," Harry said.

In the Iroquois cabin, Piano Legs Scarborough impatiently tried to get Alan Friedman, Hayden Peake, and Preston Wingo settled.

"Oh-oh," Hayden said, putting a hand on top of his head, "I left my stuff on the bus."

"I know," Piano Legs said. "Look for it in the woods. What a dumb little twerp you are."

Preston got out his books and arranged them carefully in his locker. Books were to him what snacks and horseplay were to others.

Alan Friedman, pressing his nose against the screen to look out, caused a small rip in the rusted mesh, earning him his second painful snuggy of the day from Piano Legs.

"Keep it up, Friedman," Piano Legs said, "and you'll set a first-day snuggy record."

The three nine-year-olds in the Navajo cabin were driving Curtis Kirk to distraction. Usually patient, he found it most difficult to deal with certain basic situations. In this case, Harvey Allen wanted to go to the bathroom but was afraid to leave his things alone in the cabin. Furth Sklar wanted to go too, but wouldn't go unless Clark Kent went with him. Clark didn't want to go. He didn't want to do anything but mope.

"But *somebody* should go," Curtis clucked like a mother hen, fluttering around the room trying to console the boys, "if you *need* to."

Things were somewhat less frantic in the girls' cabins. Dee Dee immediately lit up a cigarette, quickly filling the Seminole cabin with smoke. Gerri Belardi snatched the weed out of her mouth. "I don't want to see that again," she snapped.

"Don't look," Dee Dee said.

"Who's that?" asked Robin Holt, pointing to a poster being tacked up by June Grabowsky.

"Lee Majors."

"Now *there's* somebody for you to go after, Dianne," Dee Dee said.

"Not my type."

In the Cherokee cabin, Hazel Stanfield and Paper Woman started dusting and cleaning up, joined by their counselor, Stacy Brunkhorst. Following Stacy every step like a puppy was little Cathy Shimizu.

"How do you get your hair like that, Stacy?" Cathy asked.

"Oh, just keep it cut and brushed. It's a wedge."

"Oh. How do you get your hair like that, Hazel?"

Hazel looked over. "It's natural. An Afro."

"Oh. I think I'll have mine like Stacy's."

In the Hopi cabin, Michelle Hinchman claimed her territory like a landlord and eyed unfavorably Joyce Cuccinello, who had retreated to the far corner and was unpacking her dolls. Sue Lopez, a quiet and dark little girl, sat on her bunk sighing. B.J. Littlefield, the sturdy counselor, adopted her Howard Cosell voice to narrate the action:

". . . Now Joyce is standing up her Little Orphan Annie doll, just like I predicted at the top of the show . . ."

Jane Smith was helping everybody unpack and organize themselves in the Penobscot cabin, instructing them all the while on various matters of self-protection.

Dierdre Bush, a quiet, unassuming, and obedient girl easily influenced by anyone who spoke with authority, nodded continually.

"What a marvelous time we're going to have," sang Debbie Settlemire.

"Long as we don't get raped," Dierdre said.

Kiki Watwood was quickly impatient with the youngest girls in the Cheyenne cabin. Barbie Lipski turned up her nose at the unsanitary conditions, but said nothing and went about the business of cleaning up industriously.

Marian Pincu, on the other hand, chattered endlessly. "I miss my parents already," she said to Kiki, "I really do. This is not easy for me, trying to adjust. I don't like being homesick. But you know what? They're going to send me brownies and cookies every day."

"You'll get even fatter than you are already," Kiki growled. "How'd you like to end up looking like your brother?"

"I won't. These are *health food* brownies."

Lunch at the boys' dining hall was rowdy as usual, with a lot of whooping and hollering and sneaky tossing of food as the counselors tried to keep order.

"Great chow," said Clark Brunkhorst, gobbling down his second liverwurst sandwich.

"You always say that," Wolfman Hinchman said, peering at him under his beetle brows. "Then by the second week you say it's rotten chow. By the third week you can't stand it any more. It's the same chow. Ouch!" He touched the top of his head.

"What's the matter?"

"Must of hurt myself on the bus."

"Heard the one about Gale Pincu's sister?" Bobby Stenzel yelled.

"No," Hulk said. "And we're not going to."

The girls' lunch was more subdued, but Michelle Hinchman did manage to drip some tuna fish on Joyce's lap, causing a minor scene and some wet eyes on Joyce.

"Why are you always picking on me?" Joyce whined.

"Who's picking? You're handy, is all."

"You're handy too, Michelle," said B.J., standing over her, "and I'll smack you if you do that again."

"Accident."

"Yeah. My smack will be an accident too."

Several girls laughed.

After lunch everybody gathered at the council ring, where were held the nighttime fires and storytelling sessions. But now, sitting on logs in a circle, they heard the same afternoon talk Steamboat had welcomed campers with for eighteen years.

"I want you all to know," he said, pacing back and forth in the middle of the ring, his broad hands jammed in his rear pockets, looking just like a football coach giving a pregame pep talk, "that Camp Smilin' Through stands for friendship, learning camping skills, and fun. It stands for brotherhood, helping the other guy—or gal. Like they say, what goes around comes around. That means if you're helpful, people will help you, and if you're not, you won't get help from others. . . ."

If somebody else had been delivering this talk, there would have been some wise comments from the audience. But Steamboat commanded respect, just by his manner. They nodded when he asked if they understood, and laughed at his weak old jokes.

Then he asked each camper to stand and give his or her name, starting with girls, of course.

Most of the girls simply stated their names with downcast eyes and sat quickly back down. Some of the older ones, though, drew wry comments from older boys.

"Dianne Wingo."

"Dianne is a dump," muttered her brother Turkey.

But several boys eyed her appreciatively.

Michelle Hinchman drew scattered boos.

A couple of the youngest girls stood but were too shy and flustered to utter their names. Vance supplied them for the audience.

As the boys went around, the response got more raucous.

Bobby Stenzel got cheers.

Gale Pincu was greeted by his sometime nickname, "Sea Cow."

Charlie Stritzinger winced in anticipation of a mean comment, but got none at all.

Clark Brunkhorst drew cheers second only to Bobby's, and Wolfman got some too—so it always was with the athletes.

Furth Sklar rose and said he had to go to the bathroom. That unnerved Curtis Kirk, who suggested quickly that he go with Clark Kent. But Clark didn't want to go, so Curtis had to take him—a departure that brought some derisive squeals from the group.

"Now," Steamboat said when they were finished with introductions, "I suppose you've all been wondering what I had in store for you this afternoon."

There were some quiet groans from those who knew.

With Steamboat making the assignments, they went right to work—weeding, mopping floors, airing out cabins, stacking and patching canoes, and other chores.

Clark Brunkhorst took great pains to sweep and patch the asphalt sidewalk leading from the dining hall down to the dock. Then he raced over to his cabin and returned with his skateboard. He jumped on it and took a quick run the length of the walk.

"Hey!" Steamboat trotted after him. "That's not work!"

"I gotta test it, don't I?" Clark said, smiling broadly.

Michelle swished her paint brush in the air, lodging a small glob of brown on Joyce's arm, bringing renewed tears to Joyce's eyes.

"Aw, you needed some touching-up," Michelle said.

B.J. didn't see it, as she was busy narrating the play-by-play of the girls cleaning up the dining hall kitchen. "Yes, fans, as I anticipated at the top of the show, the work is actually eventuating in an improvement in the overall picture . . ."

By dusk they all were exhausted. They gobbled

down plates of franks and beans with little byplay and shenanigans.

Then, after a brief rest in their cabins, they gathered around the campfire at the council ring. Light flickered on all the eager faces. Everybody loved the campfires, the eerie and exciting flames setting off the mysterious dark of the woods at their backs.

"I want to thank you all," Steamboat said, "for the splendid jobs you did this afternoon. Camp looks great. Now I would like to announce the awards for the two hardest workers. The awards will be a good round of applause. And the recipients are—Hazel Stanfield and Gale Pincu!"

For their efforts they got mostly hoots and jeers.

Vance Brehm stood next to Steamboat, rubbing his hand over his beard and winking slyly. "The special goldbrick award," he announced, "for the least amount of work goes to Dianne Wingo and her adorable brother, Turkey. The award is a swirly!"

Everybody laughed, and Turkey pretended to run away in fright.

Dee Dee took the opportunity of the distraction to look over at Bobby Stenzel and smile. He responded with a cocky wink. She looked away haughtily, then caught Charlie Stritzinger's eye and threw him a wise, taunting smile and a come-hither wink.

Charlie's jaw dropped in disbelief.

Bobby snarled at him. "Watch it, buster."

Dianne took all this in carefully.

"Okay," Steamboat said, "I have some things to do. Vance will take over and present his first ghost story."

There were murmurs of approval and excitement.

He told the story of Crazy Wilson. Even though the older campers had heard it every year, he told it so well and so convincingly that all eyes and ears were riveted on him.

The story was this: Crazy Wilson was an Indian who lived years ago in this very woods with his wife and children. As he grew older, he began to grow crazier. He grew crazier and crazier. Finally one night he rolled a giant boulder down the hill onto his whole family, smashing them all amid horrific screaming and bloodshed. (Vance was expert at horrific screaming and acting out all parts and scenes.)

Then Crazy Wilson hanged himself with a stocking cap over his face in the front hall of his house. Now his ghost haunts the house and haunts the woods all around this camp. And his faithful dog haunts with him—the howling Hound of Death!

The little kids were terrified, and most of the older ones were well satisfied with what was always a great story excellently told.

After they got their breath and quieted down, Hulk led them in a spirited singing of the camp song, *You Can't Be Blue at Smilin' Through.*

Then the council ring broke up and tired campers drifted off.

Dianne sidled up to Vance Brehm, trying to hide the fact that she was trembling considerably. She said to him, as sexily as she could manage, "Hi, Vance."

"Hey, there, Dianne, how's it going?"

"Fine. Fine. Unh, don't you think I've . . ." she smoothed her shirt, ". . . grown?"

"Yup, sure thing. Almost big as Hulk." He smiled kindly.

"That's not what I mean," she said with deepening embarrassment and nervousness, afraid of others' eyes that might be following her actions, "and I am *not.* Do you, um, know how old I am?"

He glanced around at the departing campers. "What, about thirty?"

She blushed. "No! I'm thirteen."

"Well now, is that a fact?" He edged away. "You win the guess-Dianne's-age contest, then. I would have said thirty, maybe thirty-five. Now," he took her shoulders and turned her away, "you get going on back around the lake like a good little thirteen-year-old. Bedtime." He walked away, whistling a tune.

Dianne, hoping with all hope that no one had heard this, scampered to catch up with the other girls walking toward their cabins.

As the boys moved into their cabin area behind the dining hall, Bobby Stenzel caught up with Charlie. "Hey, skinny, don't let me catch you messing with my girl."

"I wasn't," Charlie said, his mind still on the smile and wink he had got from Dee Dee.

"Just so you don't get any ideas . . ." He gave Charlie a vicious snuggy and walked on, leaving Charlie wincing with pain.

It wasn't long before the camp was quiet. The weary youngsters dropped quickly off to sleep.

But it wasn't totally quiet. Low snickering came from the boys' waterfront as counselors Hulk, Vance, Harry, Curtis, and Piano Legs tiptoed around to take two canoes from the rack and slide them into the water.

"I don't know about this . . ." Curtis said, hesitating.

"Aw, come on," Hulk said, pulling his arm.

Carefully they climbed into the canoes and pushed off.

On the other side of the lake there was some quiet snickering too. B.J., Stacy, Gerri, Jane, and Kiki were grouped at the shore a ways off from the dock. They strained to see over the dark water in the direction from which the male counselors would come. They waited, giggling.

Annie walked softly up behind them. She didn't say a word, but waited until they saw her. When they did, none of them said anything either. In embarrassed silence they split up and went back to their cabins.

Annie still waited, her arms folded across her chest.

The only giggling left came from the lake, where the two canoes were approaching.

The canoes glided through the water, but for the

counselors' snickering they might just as well have been driving a motorboat.

They reached the shore and quickly beached the canoes.

Annie strolled over. They looked up. Without a word they quickly relaunched the canoes and headed back for their side of the lake. Annie grinned to herself.

"Well," Vance said softly after they had paddled several yards, "so much for fraternization with the opposite sex."

"She won't be waiting for us every night," Piano Legs said.

"It's not worth it," Curtis said, shaking his head.

"Would have been good for you," Hulk said.

In the darkened Seminole cabin, Dianne raised herself on her elbows and leaned toward Dee Dee's bunk. "I had a very long and serious conversation with Vance," she whispered.

"You did?"

"Yes. He told me he thinks I'm becoming very mature—and you know what *that* means."

"I'll bet he did."

"He did! You wait!"

"I'm waiting."

"We even talked about the possibilities of . . . a date!"

"Ha!"

Dianne flopped back on her pillow.

"Hey, Dianne?" whispered Robin. "Have you ever kissed a boy with a beard?"

"Lots of times."

"You have not," Dee Dee said.

"I have so."

"Who, smarty?"

"You wouldn't know them." Dianne studied her nails in the dark. "They were older guys, with customized vans."

"How does it feel to kiss a boy with a beard?" Robin asked.

"Okay."

June Grabowsky sighed. "I'd *love* to kiss Lee Majors with that sexy moustache he used to have."

"Phooey," Dee Dee said. "I'm glad he shaved it off. It looked like a yucky caterpillar crawling across his face."

"It did *not!*"

"Don't argue with me, honeybunch."

"Well, he's the Six-Million-Dollar Man."

"That and a dollar will get you another poster of him."

June lapsed into a hurt silence. She had only wanted to participate in the discussion, but with those two it just never worked.

"Well, anyway," Dianne said, "I'm having a date with Vance.

"Sure," Dee Dee said, "and I'm having one with Robert Redford."

Dee Dee lit up a cigarette just as Gerri came through the door.

"Put that out!" she barked. "And I mean *now!*"

"Okay, okay, keep your T-shirt on."

Night settled over the camp. All was still. Then suddenly a blood-curdling scream cut the silence. "Yoooooowww!"

It came from the Navajo cabin. Curtis Kirk jumped up and shook Clark Kent. "Having a bad dream?"

"Hunh? What? Where am I?"

"Right here, at camp. Everything's okay."

"Then why'd you wake me up?"

" 'Cause you screamed."

The scream brought Steamboat and Annie up in their bed in their cottage.

"Guess we got another screamer this year," Annie said, sighing.

"Yeah. Usually just the first night or two, though."

Again all was silent.

Then in the distance came an eerie howling, low at first, then rising. Like a wolf.

All through the camp eyes popped wide open. Eyes stayed open until the howling stopped.

June touched Robin's arm. "The Hound of Death," she whispered.

Robin pulled the covers up over her head.

By morning, though, all that was forgotten. Vance led calisthenics for the boys, Gerri Belardi for the girls. Piano Legs and Harry Driscoll lounged to one side of the boys' ranks, watching idly.

Hulk walked by and looked down at the two counselors. "Piano Legs, I saw you give one of your kids a snuggy when we were all getting on the bus. If you do that anymore—"

"What're you gonna do," Piano Legs said, a hint of a smile flitting over his face, "tell my old man?"

"No, I'm not gonna tell your old man. You know that's not the way I operate. I'm gonna tell *me*, and then you and me can step out in the woods and I'll give you a snuggy that'll make you a boy soprano again."

"You don't scare me, Brunkhorst." Piano Legs pulled up a few blades of grass and chewed on the ends.

"Well, come on then, let's go right now."

"I got a weak arm," Piano Legs muttered.

"Yeah, and a weak brain. Keep it in mind, what I said."

"We all gotta keep our kids in line the best way we can, Hulk."

"There are better ways than snuggies, even for you."

"Always works."

When Hulk had left, Harry laughed. "You were dumb to get caught, man."

"Don't worry about it."

Midmorning was swim time, just when the morning chill had eased and the sun burnished Drum Lake. The first thing the swimmers were ordered to do was wade out and pluck the various odd bits of small debris that surfaced daily.

Michelle tried continually to dunk Joyce, taking advantage of the fact that B.J. was occupied on the shore handing out the tags that all swimmers had to keep pinned to them while in the water.

"Lemme alone!" Joyce sputtered.

Michelle eventually got bored with that and set out for the raft, swimming with long, powerful strokes.

Standing in the shallow water where the youngest girls were splashing about, Gerri Belardi looked over the lean form of June Grabowsky, who was a good swimmer.

"You interested in track?" Gerri asked.

"I don't know. Never tried it."

"You'd be wonderful at field events. Looks like you've got good upper-body strength."

"Gee, gosh, I don't know." June blushed with delight at the attention. "Think I could?"

"You'd sure be better at it than darned old Dee Dee or Dianne."

"Gee, gosh."

Cute Stacy Brunkhorst, easing her way into the water, was as usual the subject of much admiration and envy from the younger campers, who yearned to look so good in bathing suits.

"Where'd you get your suit?" Cathy Shimizu asked.

"I don't know. It was a gift."

"I'm gonna get one like that."

On the boys' side, Bobby Stenzel challenged Sterling, Thornton, and Turkey to a race to the raft. They were not three of the stronger swimmers, and Bobby won handily.

"The trouble with this place," he said, looking around in mock annoyance, "is that there isn't any real competition." He strutted around on the raft, tightening and relaxing his arms and chest, hoping some of the girls might notice his firm muscles.

Charlie Stritzinger was not fond of swimming, any

more than of any sports. He dawdled at water's edge, not wanting to swim, yet not wanting either to avoid the water completely and thus risk being dunked by the more athletic types.

"Hey, Charlie!"

Charlie thought that Steamboat's call was for the purpose of prodding him into the water. "Yes?"

"Charlie," Steamboat said, coming up and putting an arm around him, "how'd you like to be editor of the *Shoshone?*"

"Me? Edit the paper? Really?"

"Yup. You're my man. Unless, of course"—Steamboat looked at the sky—"you'd rather spend the afternoons learning Indian lore with Curtis."

"Oh, no, Steamboat! I would *love* to do it. Gee . . ."

"We need a girl too, somebody to gather news from the girls' side. Got any ideas?"

"Well, um . . ." Charlie looked at the ground and scuffed some sand around with a bare foot. ". . . Maybe somebody like, um, just for an example, Dee Dee Keough would do a good job. I mean, unh, somebody like that."

"We'll find somebody good," Steamboat said.

CHAPTER
4

Two visitors sat rather stiffly in the small living room of the Scarborough cottage, facing Steamboat and Annie.

One was Freddy Bolin, the twenty-nine-year-old son of the former owner of the Smilin' Through land, and now himself the heir and owner. A lean and nervous man, Freddy seemed a bit uncomfortable with the way the conversation was going. But his confidence was enhanced by the presence of the second man.

That man was a strong, dark, broad-shouldered, brooding, and silent man introduced to the Scarboroughs only as "my friend and partner, Hal." Hal's eyes remained half-closed, and through them he stared at his folded hands on his lap. But his size and slouch and silence gave him an ominous air.

Freddy glanced at the ceiling, then at his hands. "My dad was a sentimental man, Steamboat. You know that. In a lot of ways he wasn't realistic enough about his business and his property holdings."

"Whereas you," Steamboat said softly, "have a real good business head and aren't burdened by sentiment."

"Hey," Freddy spread his arms, "I'm as sentimental as the next guy, Steamboat. I was a camper here myself for five years, this very place. So I have a real soft spot in my heart for old Camp Smilin' Through. But I also have a soft spot for not getting ruined in business. And this *is* a business, after all."

"Well, I guess maybe *now* it is, Freddy. But I don't think your dad saw it quite that way. To him it was something he loved. And by the way, I remember you well as a camper. You didn't socialize much as I recall."

"Well, I was never much of an athlete."

"Hmm."

"But I enjoyed it, every minute of it." He paused for a few moments. "Look, I know you don't like it," he said in a firmer voice, "but you've got to face the fact that dad's gone and now I'm the owner of this property. I've got to do what's right for my holdings."

"And you want to make a killing." Steamboat's voice firmed too.

"No, no." Freddy held up his palms innocently. "Not that at all. Not a killing, just a living. And I've had offers for this property, very, very tempting ones. And a lot of people tell me I'm an idiot to keep turning them down just because of my old summer camp —fond as I am of the memories."

"Certainly wouldn't want you to be thought of as an idiot."

"Hey, let's face it, Steamboat, the place is going to the dogs."

Annie leaned forward. "If you'd invest some money in the camp, we'd be right back in good shape."

"No, you wouldn't," Freddy said, shaking his head. "That's not realistic. Anyway, dad never sank any real money into it. The fact is you always made enough to keep the place up and pay the taxes and sometimes even show dad a little profit. But look at you now. You've only got thirty-three kids. By the time you buy the food for the summer you'll be broke."

"Don't worry about it," Steamboat said crisply. "I've got some savings."

"Hey, Steamboat." Freddy reached out and fluttered a hand in the air as if tapping him on the shoulder. "You don't want to be paying for this out of your own pocket. And I don't want to eat these property taxes. Taxes have gone up a lot. You're in a vicious circle. The big camps are killing you."

"Look, Freddy," Steamboat said pleadingly, gripping his knees hard, "if we can pay the taxes—just the taxes—will you let us hang on? How about that? Would you settle for that?"

Freddy leaned back and studied the ceiling for a minute. Then he glanced over at Hal, who still sat motionless. Then he looked at Steamboat. "Sure. Okay. You pay the taxes and we'll put off selling the land." He smiled slightly. "What the heck, condominiums will be worth even more two years from now anyway."

"And by then we'll be back on our way up, Freddy," Steamboat added quickly. "You won't need to sell. It's just a matter of time. We'll be back in the black and so will you. I've got some ideas to make the camp go better. Some ideas I've been thinking about, like—"

"Okay, okay." Freddy held up his hand. "We don't need to go into details. I'll trust you, man to man. I'll drop back up in a couple of days. You show me in your books how you can pay the taxes and we'll shake hands on it for at least another year."

"Right!" Steamboat smiled in relief. "Deal!"

The two men said their good-byes and left.

Steamboat slumped back in his chair and put his chin in his hands.

Annie shook her head slowly. "We can't tap the savings. That money is for Chet's college."

"Yeah. I'll think of something." He tried to smile at her.

Outside, Freddy and Hal trudged to their car.

"Can he do it?" Hal asked.

"Don't be ridiculous," Freddy said, smiling wryly. "I was just being easy on him. He'll never meet the tax bill on this land."

"But what if he can? I ain't gonna go easy on you for all those loans, because I ain't the slightest bit sentimental about this camp."

"Don't worry. Whatever he does, we'll make the

condominum deal. Now let's get out of here. This place has too many memories for me."

"What kind?"

"I hated camp."

At lunch, Steamboat tried to hide his depression. But some of the counselors and kids were concerned. Turkey Wingo and Clark Brunkhorst tried to get him to do his Tarzan yell—a wild whoop that always brought everybody to life and gave the campers spirit. But he shook his head.

"I don't do that anymore, boys," he said. "Hurts my throat."

Lunch went on for a while in subdued temper.

Hulk stood up. "I have an announcement to make. Camper Hayden Peake, who you all saw splashing around in the lake looking very healthy, is dead."

Hayden jumped to his feet, looking around frantically, his face ashen. "I'm not!"

"Yup, he is," Hulk said, not looking at him. "I didn't find his swimming tag back on the board. So I guess he drowned and took it with him to the bottom of the lake."

"Here it is!" Hayden waved his tag. "Right here!"

Hulk continued to ignore him. "If a guy's tag isn't on the board, he drowned. That's that. I guess we'll have to have a funeral for the poor little guy."

Trailing tears, Hayden ran out of the dining hall and down to the waterfront where he hung up his tag.

When he came back, Hulk smiled broadly at him. "Hello, Hayden, glad you didn't drown."

Hayden flushed and wiped his cheeks.

That brief episode lightened things a bit and brought the room more to life.

Turkey leaned close to Clark. "What's eating Steamboat?"

"Why?"

"He doesn't seem to be fun anymore. Look, he isn't smiling or anything. Just sitting there."

"Aw, he's okay." Clark cupped a hand over his

mouth and called, "Hey, Steamboat, you gonna try skateboarding this year?"

Steamboat shook his head.

Several boys exchanged worried looks.

Camping activities quickly settled into their routine. Afternoons included canoeing.

Among the girls, Robin Holt was one of the best. Ordinarily a little shy about participating in sports, Robin opened up in canoeing. She was slender and not apparently strong, but was very well coordinated and had smooth technique.

B.J. called for a race among Robin, Michelle, and June. Robin won by two lengths. She was grinning as she beached her canoe.

Annie came up to congratulate her, which caused Robin to blush. "Unh, Robin, ever thought about working on the *Shoshone*?"

"No, I guess not."

"Like to?"

"Well, sure, I guess."

"Interested in being the girls' editor?"

"Really? Sure! Wow, that'd be terrific." She blinked several times.

"Good," Annie said. "That's settled then. Now we have a boys' editor *and* a girls' editor."

"Who's the boy?" Robin asked casually.

"Charlie Stritzinger."

"Oh, that's nice."

"I think you'll be a good team."

"Gee, I'll sure try, Annie, thanks."

When Annie left, Robin let herself bathe in the satisfaction. She flopped down on the sand, smiling and chuckling. "Gee, girls' editor!"

At the girls' baseball game, Wolfman's sister, Michelle, dominated, slugging long hits and running the base paths with good speed. She was aggressive and tough. She became quickly annoyed when balls were dropped or fielders didn't hustle. "Nobody cares about sports, darn it!" she hollered upon coming again to the plate.

She banged out a hit to right and tried to stretch it into a double. The ball came in to Cathy Shimizu in time, but when Michelle barreled in toward second, Cathy, rather than attempt a tag, leaped out of the way.

"That's no way to play baseball!" Michelle bellowed. She chased Cathy out into center field. Jane Smith ran out from her umpire position to grab Michelle before she could tangle with the frightened Cathy.

"That's no way to play baseball either, Michelle," Jane said.

"Well, they all play like . . . like a bunch of *girls*!"

Jane winced. "I agree that sometimes they leave something to be desired. But not everybody is as big and strong as you are, Michelle."

"What's that supposed to mean? That I'm not as pretty as you?"

Jane winced again, uncomfortable at being reminded of her advantage. "No, no, not that at all. Looks have nothing to do with it." She watched Michelle stomp back to second base. Jane was aware that, no matter how unfair it was, looks did have something to do with this whole business of trying to be a woman, but she didn't know exactly what it was.

The boys were skateboarding down the asphalt walk. Many were good, but as usual Clark Brunkhorst was far and away the best. He did a handstand on the board, and everybody cheered. "Let's get some competition out here!" he hollered.

Some of the smaller boys and girls attended Curtis Kirk's Indian lore class. Curtis had war paint on and gestured enthusiastically as he talked about tepees and wampum and smoke signals.

"Indians were very tough and strong," he said.

"Like you?" somebody said.

"Sort of." Curtis was truly in his element and enjoyed the rapt attention and admiration of the small campers. At least they didn't make remarks about his pale, scrawny frame.

At night, there was the usual campfire at the council ring. Awards were handed out for the day's activities. Gale Pincu got the pigging award for his exploits at supper where, by some accounts, he had downed five helpings of goulash. Hayden Peake got the black brick for forgetting to hang up his swim tag. Counselor Gerri Belardi made a pointed speech about the evils of fighting during baseball games, causing Michelle to look at the floor and mutter.

But as soon as Gerri finished, Michelle reached over and knocked Joyce Cuccinello off the log, managing to look innocent.

Vance Brehm asked the new campers to raise their hands. A handful of small boys and girls did so immediately. Vance gave a sardonic laugh, drawing some expectant giggles from the older campers, who suspected what was coming.

"You're not a real Smilin' Through camper," he said soberly, "until you've had your initiation. Until you've met . . . the ghost of Crazy Wilson!"

The new campers' expressions quickly turned to fright as Vance gave another mean laugh.

"And that will be tonight!"

Steamboat and Annie were in bed. He lay wide awake, his hands clasped behind his head, staring into the darkness.

Annie opened her eyes. "Can't sleep?"

"Thinking."

She paused a moment. "Steamboat, this has always been a kind of well-to-do kids' camp, hasn't it?"

"No more than any other. Less than most. But more or less, yeah, I guess so. You know, those who can afford the four hundred bucks. So what?"

"Never any poor kids."

"Well, you have to pay your way, don't you? This

isn't a charity camp. I'm not some do-good money-bags, you know. But I never kept anybody out whether they were Protestant or Jewish or Catholic or black or white—as opposed to some camps I could mention."

"You don't have to tell *me* that, Steamboat. But how would you feel about a few poor black and Spanish kids coming out here?"

"Kids are kids. I like 'em all. Just as long as they have the four hundred bucks. I'm not in a position to give it away, like I said. Wish I was." He turned to her, "What are you driving at anyway?"

"Just a thought I had. Maybe nothing worthwhile."

"Look, if a *Martian* kid wanted to come out here and he could pay his freight, I wouldn't care. You know any Martians?"

"Try to get some sleep."

"Yeah. But do you know any Martians?"

"Maybe."

Vance led the group of small campers through the winding trail in the dark woods. He and B.J. led the procession with flashlights. Pines groaned in the slight breeze, and underbrush crackled beneath their feet. The new campers huddled together and shivered as they moved cautiously ahead.

A few yards behind, several of the older campers giggled as they followed those younger ones about to be initiated.

Dee Dee, still intent on her secret teasing, sidled up to Charlie. "I wish *I* was going to work on the paper with you," she said.

"Unh, oh, I wish you were too." Charlie turned crimson. "I suggested you." He blushed even more deeply. His insides bubbled with delight at her fraudulent attention.

Dee Dee and Dianne giggled together.

Bobby Stenzel was not amused. He glared at Charlie.

They approached a steep, long hill at the bottom of which was a boulder that towered over their heads.

Vance stepped up to the boulder and faced the campers, turning his flashlight to light his face hideously from below. "This was the boulder Crazy Wilson rolled onto his wife and children," he said ominously, his voice like a moan, "and it crushed them. There was blood and guts all over the ground around here."

"Watch out!" B.J. yelled. "You're standing in some blood!"

The small kids danced frightfully this way and that, as if trying to keep both feet off the ground at once.

"Yes," Vance went on softly, flicking his light up the hill, "up there is where Crazy Wilson's ghost still roams in the night." He played his beam up to the top of the hill to a ramshackle, abandoned two-story house. "Now, if you're going to be a Smilin' Through camper, you pitiful specimens who are new here have to go up on that porch and knock on that door."

They huddled together, shaking, staring up at the house in dread.

"And you say, 'Come out, come out, Crazy Wilson.' "

"What . . . what if he comes out?" Furth Sklar asked in a quaking voice.

"Then we'll all *die*," Vance intoned in a sepulchral voice.

"But he almost never does," B.J. added quickly, lest the children become too frightened to try.

"*Almost* never," Clark Brunkhorst called from the rear.

All the counselors played their beams on the house. Clark Kent started to cry, and Curtis leaned over to comfort him.

"He's gotta do it," Vance commanded. "Now, all you new campers, get going!"

Almost as scared of the counselors as of Crazy Wilson by now, the knot of new campers scrambled up the hill to the porch.

"Knock!"

Nobody dared approach the door.

"Okay, we're leaving you here!"

The counselors turned off their flashlights. Sobbing came from the porch. They turned their lights back on.

"Do it!" Vance roared.

Huddled together piteously, they tiptoed onto the porch.

"Knock, you useless cowards!"

Barbie Lipski, the only one of the new campers who dared suspect that somehow it might be a joke, knocked.

Nothing happened.

"Say it!" Vance yelled.

"Crazy Wilson, come out!" Barbie called, her voice trembling.

For a moment, nothing happened.

Then the window shade in the door snapped up with a loud clatter and a horrible figure appeared in the doorway, a stocking cap pulled down over his eyes and a noose dangling around his neck. The figure groaned.

The kids screamed, spun around, and rolled and tumbled down the hill, scrambled to their feet, and tore off through the woods for camp—along with the old campers, who were almost as scared, even though they knew it was only Hulk in the doorway.

Charlie was trotting along toward the rear of the pack when Bobby grabbed his arm, whirled him around, and without a word, punched him in the nose.

Charlie crumpled to the ground as Bobby trotted on.

Robin Holt knelt beside him. "Are you all right?"

"Aside from the fact that I'll never smell again," he said bravely, "I'm fine." He pushed her away, afraid he was going to cry.

She watched him run off, then ran after him.

Up at the old house, Vance, B.J., and Hulk stood in the crumbling living room, laughing at the success of the annual Crazy Wilson initiation rite. Hulk pulled off his stocking cap and scratched his itching face.

Suddenly there was a thumping noise overhead. They froze.

"What was that?" B.J. whispered.

"Just one of the gang, probably Driscoll," Hulk said, a bit anxiously. He went over to the broken stairwell and called up, "Who's up there? That you, Harry?"

From upstairs, there was a moan, then a clanking sound as if a chain were being rattled.

The three counselors looked at each other wide-eyed.

Then, above them, they heard the ungodly howl.

"The Hound of Death!" B.J. wailed.

They burst out of the house and raced toward camp, hearing again the weird howling behind them.

CHAPTER
5

The baseball field echoed with grunts and puffs as all boys and girls together were led in calisthenics by Vance Brehm. Vance worked them hard. The better athletes kept up, but those like plump Gale Pincu just huffed and puffed, trying but not succeeding. Some of the older girls just pretended to be doing them.

"Down!" Vance hollered, flopping down into a push-up position. Most copied him. "Up and running!" They ran in place.

Bobby, Clark, Mike, and Turkey managed with no problem, and seeing their excellent condition made Vance even more exuberant.

"Higher with those knees! Higher!"

They pumped their knees.

"Now! Something new! *Kamikaze!*" This time, instead of flopping down into a push-up position on his hands, he leaped high into the air, arms and legs spread-eagled, and came down directly on his belly.

The campers gasped. Vance got up, red-faced but smiling.

"That's it" he said, his midsection obviously smarting and nearly causing him to double over. "That's the kamikaze. That's what will replace the belching contests this year. Those of you brave enough to try can try it here. But it's really meant for the lake. That's where the competitions will be. Anybody want to try?"

Wolfman tried one but hit knees first. Bobby broke

his fall with his hands. Even June Grabowsky, her confidence buoyed by Gerri Belardi's encouragement to try track, tried a kamikaze, but she landed ignominiously on her rear.

Vance did another successful one, and everybody gave him an enthusiastic cheer for his demonstration of Smilin' Through's new heroic exercise feat.

"Okay," Vance said, jumping to his feet but now allowing himself to rub his reddened belly, "that's it. But from now on at the council ring there'll be an award for the best lake kamikaze of the day. At the end of camp there'll be a big award for the kamikaze of the year—and that's going to have to be a *great* kamikaze. I mean, an awe-inspiring kamikaze!"

"Like this?" Turkey Wingo said. He flung himself into the air and landed almost flat on his stomach in the sand, groaning.

"No. That was only a *fair* kamikaze. To win for the year, it has to be a kamikaze that will stop the world!"

They roared approval.

"Now! In addition to the usual program for the morning, there will be unstructured activity with me on the beach from ten to eleven. Volunteers only. Let's go to regular activities, then this afternoon we'll get to the lake and work on those kamikazes!"

Charlie Stritzinger sat at a large desk in the back room of the Scarborough cottage. He was wearing an old-fashioned green eyeshade much too large for him, and occasionally it slid down over his eyes.

In one corner of the desk was an ancient typewriter, and in another was an equally ancient mimeograph machine. On the walls were old copies of the *Shoshone*, the two-page mimeographed camp newspaper.

"Nice eyeshade," Annie said, walking into the room. "Where'd you find it?"

"Under some stuff over there." He frowned. "I don't know how to type."

"That's what I'm here for. I'm your chief flunky, typist, and bottle-washer around here. You work up the stories, just give 'em to me to type finished. So you get busy now and write up a nice welcome to the new campers." She lay a sheet of paper on the desk in front of him. "Here's a list of everybody, along with a little bit about each one. You can also write up how the kids fixed up the camp—if you want."

Charlie blinked. "Gee, that's a lot of work."

"It'll go quickly. You're the editor, aren't you?"

"Right." He bent over the roster.

Robin Holt came in carrying a few sheets of paper. "I've got some items about the girls' side."

Charlie immediately assumed his editor's status. "Okay," he said stiffly. He waited for Annie to leave. Then he said, "I probably ought to tell you, Robin, that I requested Dee Dee Keough."

"Why?"

"Because she's, um, experienced."

Robin giggled, covering her mouth with her hand.

"I didn't mean it that way," he said testily. "Look." He slapped down his pencil. "If you're going to be on my staff, there's no time for laughing and giggling around here. This is a newspaper office."

"Well," Robin said, trying to control herself, "Dee Dee's too busy worrying about shaving her legs, so I'll have to do."

"What do you mean, shaving her legs?"

"Something you wouldn't understand—yet."

Charlie looked away in angry embarrassment. He was not assuming control the way he'd planned. "Is that your big news item, about Dee Dee?" he asked sarcastically.

"No. Mine is that my counselor, Gerri Belardi, is going to run in the Boston Marathon, and Hazel Stanfield is the Go Fish champion of the girls' camp."

"Geez!" Charlie rolled his eyes and clutched his head. "Big deal. All right, all right, get to work."

"Can I have one of those funny green things to wear on my head?"

"No! Only the editor-in-chief gets this. And it's not funny, it's important, to keep from getting eye strain."

"From what?"

"Geez! From looking at things! Stories! Editing!"

"Oh. Okay." She sat down, and they both went to work on their articles.

In the parking lot, a sheriff's car drove up. Steamboat came out to meet it.

"Hi, sheriff."

"Good to see you again, Steamboat. How're things?"

"Fine, fine. What brings you around?"

"Just came up to see how you're doing."

They leaned against the car and looked off at the camp.

"The truth is, sheriff, we're doing a little poorly this year. Not as many campers as usual. Things are a little tight."

"Sorry to hear it. By the way, I also wanted to give you a friendly warning." The sheriff took his elbow. "We think the old hermit's going a little crazy for real maybe, and we're making an effort to find him and maybe keep an eye on him."

"Crazy Wilson? Naw, he never hurt anybody. We never even see him anymore. He's even part of the legend about ghosts around here." Steamboat chuckled. "Wow, if the kids knew there really was a Crazy Wilson out there, they'd all go home tomorrow!"

"Well, I certainly don't want to interfere with your legend. And he's always been harmless, I know. But there's been some stealing from farms around here, some small animals missing."

"Maybe coyotes?"

"Maybe and maybe not. Looked more like the work of some human to us. The only known human around here that we can't account for is the old Indian. We think maybe he's getting senile and a little dangerous —you know, from being alone all these years. So do me a favor, and yourself too. Keep an eye on your kids. If anything or anybody turns up missing, let me know immediately. We'll be on Crazy Wilson so fast he'll think he really *did* roll a boulder on his family."

"He really did," Steamboat said, smiling coyly.

"You're getting senile yourself," the sheriff said, chortling. "Well, gotta be getting back."

The sheriff left, and Steamboat headed back for his cottage. "He's not *that* crazy," he mumbled.

Afternoon was bright and warm. Vance lay up against a tree, chewing on a blade of grass as he watched a bunch of boys working in front of him.

They wielded sticks and were thumping them against the sand, across which lay two brand-new pairs of Levis.

"Keep it up," Vance called. "Get them jeans good and soft for me. Can't wear 'em stiff, you know. Makes me cranky to go around in stiff new jeans. And you don't want me cranky, do you?"

They groaned and muttered and grumbled while they whacked the jeans with the sticks. But for all that, they were smiling and chuckling. Doing things for their favorite counselor was not unpleasant duty —especially when the alternative was to go to Curtis Kirk's handicraft class.

The girls were playing baseball. Little Debbie Settlemire swung at Michelle's pitch and tapped a slow roller. Running to first base, she tripped and fell.

"Ooow," she moaned, clutching her ankle.

Her Counselor, Kiki Watwood, watching bored from the sidelines, muttered, "Clumsy little jerk."

But B.J. interrupted her Howard Cosell commentary immediately and rushed out to see if Debbie was all right; she was joined by Stacy.

"Just turned it a little," Debbie said, sniffling, as she got to her feet and limped off.

Michelle kicked the ground with disgust. "Baby," she growled.

Stacy went over to Kiki and stood over her, hands on hips. "Kiki, you darned well better start paying a little attention to your girls. Debbie's one of yours, you know. If you don't shape up, I'll have to tell Annie."

"What am I supposed to do, run to first base for her?"

"No, but you could have gone out there to see if she was okay."

"Next time."

Gerri Belardi used the break in the game to go over to Paper Woman. "With your slender build I think you would make a good distance runner."

"Or a good bookmark," Paper Woman said.

"Think about it."

"Okay."

Activities went on around the camp. Some of the girls were canoeing. Jane Smith tried to teach the smaller girls the style of dipping the paddle into the water, pulling it back smoothly, then turning it so that the blade kept the canoe moving straight ahead.

Dee Dee and Dianne were goofing off together, trying not to be noticed. But B.J., ambling over from the baseball game, spotted them behind the canoes.

"Either baseball or canoeing or leaf-printing class, you two."

"Do we have to?" Dee Dee groaned.

"I think I'll send you to leaf-printing class with Curtis."

They looked at each other. "We'll play baseball," Dee Dee said.

They wandered over to the baseball field and immediately lay down in right field. Michelle started for them angrily. Stacy restrained her.

"Just worry about your pitching," Stacy said.

On the boys' side another baseball game was in

progress. Gale Pincu tried to catch a pop-up in left field but the ball hit him on the head.

"You'll get the black brick for that, Sea Cow!" Bobby yelped.

"Get somebody who can play left field," Clark moaned.

"Shoot," Turkey said, spitting in the dirt, "we ain't got anybody who can play."

"Bunch of feebleminded nerds we got this year," Wolfman complained. "Sure do miss Smitty and the Rock."

Harry Driscoll was running archery practice. Thornton, Paper Man, and some of the little kids were gathered around testing their bows. Alan Friedman put an arrow in his bow to get ready, but accidentally launched it, missing Harry by inches. Harry gave him a quick and efficient snuggy.

"Ow! Sorry." Alan straightened out his pants.

"You almost became a murderer, dummy," Harry said.

Hayden Peake stepped up and aimed at the target. He was so weak that he sent the arrow a scant ten feet before it wobbled to the ground.

"If you had a moose standing right in front of you," Harry said, "you might shoot him in the toe, if you were lucky."

"Moose?" Hayden looked around nervously.

"Plenty of them in these woods. And they might get you. Better learn to shoot that arrow."

Tears came to Hayden's eyes.

Paper Man managed to reach the target with his arrow—or at least the straw on which the target was pinned.

"Not bad, Paper Man. But the way you're built, you might be better off letting the arrow shoot *you*."

Indeed, on his next shot, Paper Man pulled the string so hard he launched himself backward.

A few of the boys were skateboarding. But without

Clark Brunkhorst, who was playing baseball, it was not the same. They kept falling off.

Steamboat ambled by. Sterling and Charlie asked him to join them.

"Not now or *ever*," Steamboat said, waving them off. "I'm too old."

"Aw, you're not old, Steamboat," Sterling said. "To be old, you gotta be as old as Crazy Wilson."

"Well, I'm not that old, but I'm not that crazy either. You guys go ahead. Anybody see Chet?"

"Who? Oh, you mean—" Charlie stopped himself from saying Piano Legs. "I think maybe he went up to his cabin."

"What're you wearing that green eyeshade for, Charlie? You still working?"

"Oh, this?" Charlie fingered the shade and blushed. "Just forgot to take it off, I guess."

In the Iroquois cabin, Preston Wingo sneaked in alone, reached under his mattress, and pulled out a book—a Hardy Boys mystery. He quickly left the cabin and dashed off into the woods. He followed a path familiar to him until he came to a man-sized culvert. He stooped and entered. A few feet in he came to his log, sat down on it, leaned back against the wall of the pipe, sighed happily, and settled in to read.

He became, as usual, thoroughly absorbed in his reading. Until he heard a slight rustling at the mouth of the pipe. He looked up to see Piano Legs's face, on which was a mean smile.

Piano Legs beckoned to him with a finger. Preston scrambled out of the pipe. Piano Legs grabbed his arm and hauled him back to camp—directly to the lavatory.

"If you yell," he said to the squirming boy, "I'm really gonna fix you." He dragged him over to the toilet, stuck his head in the bowl, and flushed.

Preston struggled mightily, finally coming up sputtering and coughing from his swirly.

Then a shadow fell over them both. It was Steamboat's shadow. He stood in the doorway, hands on hips, eyes narrowed. "What's going on?"

"Oh, hi, dad," said Piano Legs, instantly releasing his hold on Preston. "His, unh, er, face was dirty."

"Are you all right, Preston?" Steamboat asked, coming in.

"Oh, sure, Steamboat," Preston said, his face dripping. He smiled weakly. "Fine."

"Get on out to the ballfield, Preston."

"Sure. Great." He scampered off.

"Now, Chet."

"Yes, sir?"

"Sometimes you're a disgrace." Steamboat stood facing him, hands on hips, jaw set. "What's the matter with you, boy? Why do you do this kind of stuff? Tell me!"

For a moment Piano Legs looked at the floor. Then he clenched his fists at his side and looked up at his father, glaring through wet eyes. "You and your dumb camp!"

"What?" Steamboat's mouth fell open.

"It's all you care about! You like the other counselors better than me!"

"No, that's not—"

"You like *everybody* better'n me!"

"No, that's not—"

"You like the other football players better than me!"

"What are you saying? That's not true." Steamboat was shocked.

"Then why was I always third string? Why ain't I head counselor instead of Brunkhorst? Hunh? Answer me that!"

Steamboat was confused. He stammered. "I just always played the best players. Don't you understand? And you don't deserve to be head counselor, not doing this kind of stuff. Can't you understand that? You have to *deserve* what you get."

"Then what do I deserve? Nothing!"

"That's not what I—"

"You like the other boys better!"

"No!" Steamboat shook his head rapidly, trying to restrain his rage and frustration and sort through the words to say what he meant. "They just *do* better than you. Now listen here! If you *ever* do another cruel thing to a boy at this camp, if I even hear you *talk* about giving somebody a swirly, I'll, I'll—I'll fire you!"

"I quit!" Piano Legs turned to walk out.

"No, you don't! You can't quit! I'm not letting you quit! You're my son! Now get back to work!"

Piano Legs stormed past him, leaving Steamboat panting and alone.

Steamboat was very upset, concerned, confused, frustrated. He felt deeply guilty in a way he couldn't quite understand, couldn't quite figure out. He never seemed to say exactly what he meant to Chet. Never seemed to quite break through the veil of hostility that separated them. He loved his son, but wasn't reaching him.

He went to his cottage to calm down, hoping somehow that his threat and directive would straighten Chet out. He had so many things on his mind.

But the first thing Piano Legs did upon leaving the lavatory was to go into the Sioux cabin and put a handful of dirt into Hulk Brunkhorst's cot.

It was dance night, and in the boys' dining hall Annie was playing records that featured slow dance stuff from the fifties. Very few kids or counselors were dancing—and most of the couples dancing were girls. Boys stood against the wall making snide comments.

The exception was Dee Dee and Bobby, who cut some neat figures to the slow, big-orchestra music. When Bobby finished up a number by doing a deep dip, cradling Dee Dee in one arm, there were some mocking hoots from the sidelines.

Finally B.J. relieved Annie at the record player and put on some livelier music—the Beatles and Rolling Stones and Santana. The change in musical mood drew lots more people onto the floor. Hulk did a heavy but spirited solo that brought some cheers. Vance and Stacy did a good hustle and were copied by many of the campers. Paper Woman shyly asked Gale Pincu to dance.

Reluctantly, he agreed, but besides being twice her size, Gale was three times as clumsy. Sideline jibes quickly forced him off the floor, and he retreated to a lonely corner to sulk.

Paper Woman went back to dancing with Hazel.

Harry Driscoll danced with Jane Smith. Jane, at her prettiest in a long dress (with a button saying, "Support the Equal Rights Amendment" pinned over her heart), was smooth and smiling.

During a pause, Harry whispered to her, "We'll be over later."

Vance left the dance floor to go out to the kitchen and tend the roasting hot dogs. Dianne quickly followed him, stood demurely behind him trying to gather her wits, and was about to speak when her brother Turkey came in and shoved her away.

"We don't need no smelly girls cluttering up our kitchen," Turkey barked.

She looked at Vance. "He just doesn't understand us."

"Hunh?" Vance was busy with the hot dogs.

Turkey did a mincing step around the kitchen, mimicking her. "Oh, Vance, he doesn't *understand*! You're putrid, Dianne."

"Vance," she said very softly, "you and I can talk later."

"What?"

But she was gone.

"I can't stand her," Turkey said to Vance. "Some

guys think she's cute, but she's just dumb, and *man* is she mean."

"Big sisters seem like that sometimes, little buddy," Vance said, turning the hot dogs.

By now the dance was turning silly, the boys mocking the girls and the girls stomping their feet and folding their arms and turning away huffily.

It was a relief to everybody when Vance announced that the hot dogs were ready.

Later that night Hulk, Harry, and Vance paddled their canoes silently across the lake—taking care this time not to engage in the chatter and laughter that had brought Annie out before to ruin their rendezvous. They beached the canoes and met Stacy, B.J., Jane, and Kiki. The boys uncovered two six-packs of sodas and they all sat down together to relax.

For a while they traded views on how the camp was deteriorating, and how sad it was, and how awful it would be if it closed.

They they turned to some mild flirtations. In the romantic moonlight, B.J. engaged in some affectionate shoulder-punching with Hulk. Vance exchanged some tentative hand-pats with Stacy, who always kept a wary eye on her protective brother, Hulk. Jane lightly tousled Harry's hair. Harry leaned his shoulder against Kiki's shoulder—not because he wasn't interested in Jane, but because she was so pretty and yet so much into women's lib that the combination of her charms and energies intimidated him.

But it was all rather forced and idle, and soon the talk drifted around to Crazy Wilson.

"I don't think he exists," Jane said.

"I think he does," said B.J. "And I've heard he may be dangerous."

"I heard that too," Vance said.

"Yeah," offered Hulk, "and we heard some darned strange sounds in his old house the other night."

"Baloney," Harry scoffed, spitting on the sand. "Mice is what you heard."

"Mice don't howl," Hulk said.

Vance sighed. "Well, I personally hope it's baloney. In any event, nobody ever sees him."

"Steamboat doesn't say it's baloney," Jane said.

"But he doesn't say it's real, either."

"Steamboat doesn't say much of anything lately," said Hulk.

They all nodded.

"Why do you suppose?"

"Who knows?" Harry said. "And who cares?"

"We all do," Hulk said. "Or we all *should*, Harry, my boy."

"Nothing we can do about it."

"We can try to be good counselors, at least."

"What a pain."

Not far from the regular camp facilities was the area for the latest camp-out, and the kids happily pitched their pup tents and pitched into the various survival chores led by their counselors. Hulk directed some of the younger ones in the art of building a fire. Vance took others to the stream where they learned to fish Indian style, dangling their lines from their fingers. Only Vance caught anything, but his pair of good-sized trout promised that at least they wouldn't starve.

Gerri Belardi led some of her girls on a pathfinding expedition, teaching them to leave and read trail signs. B.J. and Curtis combined talents to erect a sort of wigwam shelter.

Not all the kids participated. Dee Dee stayed behind to eat candy bars rather than be bored pathfinding. Preston Wingo hid in his tent, reading. Charlie and Robin sat by the fire having an "official" discussion about possible news items coming from the camp-out.

At dusk, Vance went deeper into the woods by himself, looking for just the right kind of dry firewood over which to fry his trout. Thinking himself alone, he took out a cigarette and lit it.

Then he found himself face-to-face with Dianne.

"Hello, Vance," she said in a fluttering voice.

"How ya doin' there, Dianne."

After a long pause, during which both scuffed their feet uncomfortably, Dianne said softly, "We can both talk freely now, Vance."

"Oh, yeah?" He smiled.

"I just love your beard." She didn't look at him.

"Really? Well, it keeps my chin warm."

"We, um, we can both say what's on our minds, Vance."

"Well," he cleared his throat, "I see. That is, what's on my mind just now is getting back with this firewood. Lot of hungry kids waiting. You take care now." He scooped up an armload of branches and started back.

"It was wonderful being alone with you," she suddenly blurted.

"Sure. Gotta run." He actually ran.

The next morning most of the kids were lethargic, recovering slowly from the rigors of the camp-out. An old Chevrolet pulled into the parking lot, and from it stepped a pleasant-looking, long-haired young man.

Annie and Steamboat walked over to meet him.

"I'm looking for Steamboat Scarborough," he said.

"That's me."

Annie smiled as if not surprised to see the man.

"My name's Green. I'm a social-welfare supervisor for the county." The man brushed some dust off his jacket.

"We're not quite ready for welfare yet, Mr. Green," Steamboat said, chuckling. "Next month, maybe."

"No, sir. Of course not. Mrs. Scarborough called me yesterday to say you might be interested in taking on some disadvantaged children."

Steamboat looked at her. "Really? I don't know

what got into my wife. We're practically disadvantaged ourselves. We can barely afford to feed the measly thirty-three kids we've already got. So I don't see how—"

"I see you don't understand, Mr. Scarborough. You see, these kids I'm talking about—mainly orphans from various institutions and some poorer foster homes—are very hard to place. A lot of camps won't take them."

"I didn't say I *won't* take them," Steamboat said, "I said I *couldn't* take them. I'm sorry for your kids, and I sure wish I could help them out, but I can't. So I don't know what my wife had in—"

"But let me finish, Mr. Scarborough. The county will pay *you*. Five hundred dollars per child for your three-week session— or actually a little better than *two* weeks as it now works out."

"What?" Steamboat took a step backward, his hand on his forehead. "What? Pay me? Well, why the devil didn't you say so in the first place?"

"I assumed your wife had—"

"Send me some orphans! How many you got?"

"Hundreds, believe me." Green smiled broadly. "But we did a little checking up, and we feel you could comfortably handle, say, twenty children. The grant would be ten thousand dollars."

"Ten thou—"

"Which I think would allow you to amply care for the children and not take a loss."

"Send me the orphans!" Steamboat danced a jig around the car. "Send me the orphans!"

"I'm pleased to see that you're so—"

"Mr. Green," Steamboat took the man by the shoulders, beaming, "you just saved my life!"

It was Curtis Kirk's big night to perform his Indian bonfire ceremony. While the smaller kids stared on with awe and delight, some of the larger ones snickered as Curtis, garbed in his finest fringed Indian togs and streaked with war paint, began his dance. He moved around the unlit fire, slowly at first, grunting and groaning in low, guttural, Indian-type tones.

Dianne and Dee Dee, sitting as usual at the back of the circle, were paying no attention at all.

"You did *what*?" Dee Dee asked, wrinkling her brow skeptically.

"Like I said, we met secretly in the woods. We spent a long time together. And he asked me for a date."

"For when?"

"Unh, when we get back home."

"And?"

"I said I'd think about it."

Dee Dee mused for a minute. "Hogwash."

"What's that supposed to mean?"

"It means I don't believe you were alone with Vance in the woods. And even if you were, I'll bet the only thing you said to him was 'Gee, Vance, I just *love* your beard.' "

Dianne's eyes flashed anger. "I don't care what you believe! You can just shut up! Next time we're going to kiss, and then we'll get engaged!"

"My name is Farrah."

Dianne went into a pout. But now all attention was drawn to Curtis Kirk, who had raised the level of his incantations and increased the pace of his dance around the pile of wood.

What supposedly was not known by anyone but Curtis and the other counselors was that Curtis had rigged up some electrical wires that would, at the proper time, ignite the kerosene-soaked wood and produce an instant, magical, roaring fire.

Now, at the height of his dance and chant, Curtis deftly touched the wires together with his feet.

But instead of flames leaping up, there was a loud, sooty *whooomp!* Curtis was covered from head to foot with black ash. He stood stunned, his eyes wide and staring. Most of the campers stared at him, equally stunned.

But Bobby and Turkey clutched each other, roaring with laughter.

"What did you guys *do*?" Sterling asked urgently.

"Just filled his old fire with gunpowder we got out of some of Steamboat's shotgun shells," Bobby said between gulps of laughter. "That's all."

Steamboat, Hulk, and Vance quickly checked Curtis to see that he wasn't hurt in any way—except in his pride—then led him over to a seat on the log.

Curtis slumped down, completely bewildered and disappointed.

"Well, campers," Steamboat said, "I'm sure you all enjoyed that little, unh, demonstration. Now I have an announcement to make. We will soon be joined by twenty new campers."

Reaction spread quickly through the circle, most of it positive. "More kids" "More competition!" "Better teams!" "Make 'em go to Crazy Wilson's house!"

Steamboat waited a moment for it to die down. "Twenty orphans are coming out here from the city."

Now the reaction was damped. Campers looked at each other, puzzled. "Orphans?"

"I want you to give these kids, who haven't had your advantages, a real Camp Smilin' Through welcome when they get here tomorrow," Steamboat went on. "Now, let's give the old cheer!"

And to the delight of everybody, Steamboat gave his famous Tarzan yell. The kids erupted into a tremendous cheer, not because he had directed them to, but because his enthusiasm told them the old Steamboat had returned, and that was the best news in a long time.

The morning swim on both sides of the lake was highlighted by hearty kamikaze dives off the docks. Under the supervision of B.J. on the girls' side and

Vance on the boys', the kids took off on long, soaring leaps, complete with airplane sounds or squeals or Tarzan yells, to land as flat on their bellies as possible in the lake.

Clark Brunkhorst performed best among the boys, which was a slight surprise. But on the girls' side there was much surprise over Paper Woman's heroic winner. She made a fine splat in the water that drained the color from the face of the usual winner, Michelle.

"It's easy if you're so skinny," Michelle muttered.

But among the counselors, most of the interest centered on the pending arrival of the new campers.

"Poor little things," Stacy said, "with no money and no homes."

"I hope there's no trouble," B.J. said, "you know, mixing those kids in. I hope our kids can handle it."

"Some of the new kids will probably be black," Jane said.

Hazel Stanfield had been listening in and now put both hands on her neat Afro in distress. "Blacks?" She looked scared.

"Aren't you black yourself?" Jane asked.

"Well, yeah, but . . ."

Vance and some of the other counselors expressed some concerns about possible difficulties. "Kids from such different backgrounds often have problems figuring each other out," he said.

But Curtis thought it would be, as he said, "a wonderful opportunity to bring Indian lore and handicraft skills to children who have never had the opportunity of experiencing them."

"You sound like a brochure," Harry said.

"It might be harder than you think, Curtis," Vance said. He looked at him with narrowed eyes and a slight smile. "In fact, I think you'll be lucky to escape with your life."

"Relationships are tough enough around here already," Piano Legs said. "By the way, Vance," he said with a wry smile, "does that smart little Dianne have a thing for you, by any chance?"

"Don't be ridiculous."

"I've heard it around."

"Hey," Hulk said, darting his eyes nervously around, "don't even *say* things like that about such a nice little girl."

"Actually," Vance said, "I was thinking that *Stacy* and I might make a nice couple."

"Hey," Hulk said, his face turning red, "don't even *say* things like that about my sister!"

In the back room of the Scarborough cottage, Charlie and Robin waited anxiously while Annie finished typing the first issue of the paper. They had killed the story about Gerri Belardi running in the Boston Marathon ("Not local enough," Charlie had suggested) and substituted the big news item of the day—"Orphans Arrive!"

By lunchtime word had spread around the camp that a few of the orphans might be black.

"*I* sure don't want a whole camp full of black kids," Bobby said.

"Me neither," Thornton Stanfield added, as oblivious to his own color as was his sister.

"But maybe some of 'em will be halfway decent athletes," said Wolfman.

"Yeah, they usually are," Bobby said.

"Not always," Thornton corrected.

"That's obvious," Bobby said, looking at him scornfully.

In the girls' dining hall, Annie stressed the importance of kindness and sharing. "I want you all to remember," she told the girls, "that we've had advantages these kids haven't had, and we have to make them feel a part of the group."

"We've got to make the new girls understand that they're just as good as boys," said Jane Smith, the eternal feminist.

to think about." He turned to his group. "Hey, Dog-breath! Give the dude something to think about!"

The little white boy pushed to the front of the crowd, tossed back his disheveled, dirty blond hair, leaned forward, and emitted a powerful breath right in Bobby's face.

Bobby stumbled backward, gagging and holding his nose.

Traces of the boy's foul breath spread over the other campers, who winced and held their noses as the orphans laughed.

Steamboat quickly pulled out his roster sheet and made cabin assignments, and the groups split up to follow their counselors.

In the Sioux cabin, Hulk stood as a buffer between Luscious and Bobby. Charlie, Sterling, and Gale hud-dled off in a corner.

Hulk looked at the two boys to either side of him. "Either one of you bozos wanna fight me?"

Luscious cocked his head. "You wouldn't pick on somebody younger than you, man."

"You wanna find out the hard way, bozo?" Hulk drew himself up to his full six feet four and puffed out his chest.

Luscious didn't answer.

Hulk gave the boys a hard smile. "Now, we've got baseball and swimming and lots of great ways to work off excess energy around here. Fighting ain't one of the ways."

One of the orphans, a slender, black-haired boy named Pachuco Ortiz, one of the Chicanos, calmly pulled a cigar from his shirt pocket and lit it. Hulk snatched it out of his mouth and ground it casually in his huge fist.

"Hey, man," Ortiz said, "I cut guys in East L.A. for messing with me."

"Oh, yeah?" Hulk grabbed him by the waist, flipped him upside down, and shook him by the ankles. More cigars, his knife, and a yo-yo fell from the boy's pockets.

Hulk put him down and handed him back the yo-yo. "I don't think you can cut anybody with that. Now then." He gave everybody a stern look that thoroughly cowed them. "You guys behave yourselves. I darned well mean it!"

"We're hip," Luscious said with awe in his voice.

Gerri Belardi moved Bad Henrietta Seeds, a tall, strong black girl, and Darlene Chavez, a nervous Chicano, into the Seminole cabin. Darlene was frightened of everything, including the camp and Henrietta. Bad Henrietta was as big as Gerri, which made her half a head taller than any of the other girls, and wore a perpetual scowl.

Gerri pointed Henrietta to an empty cot, but she turned toward another.

"I want *that* one," Bad Henrietta said, pointing to Dee Dee's bunk.

Without a word Dee Dee started quickly moving her stuff from her bunk.

Bad Henrietta sat on the bunk and lit a cigarette.

"No smoking," Gerri said.

Bad Henrietta continued puffing as if nothing had been said.

Gerri shrugged. Dee Dee, Dianne, Robin, and June stared at the new girl as if waiting for an order.

It came. "Set yourselves down and relax," Bad Henrietta said, "and things go a lot easier for you."

In the Choctaw cabin, Wolfman Hinchman and Clark Brunkhorst looked wonderingly at two new additions, "Burrito-Face" Rodriguez and Bad Henry Seeds, Henrietta's younger brother.

"Unh, you guys play baseball?" Wolfman asked tentatively.

"Does Joe Morgan?" Bad Henry replied, looking at him with sleepy eyes. "I am a bad, bad baseball player. Yeees. I'll spike you upside the head. I'll tag you in the mouth. I'll hit line drives off your rear ends."

"You'll get your chance," Wolfman said gruffly.

They eyed each other. Bad Henry was not large, but compactly built, and moved lithely. Burrito-Face was not big either. His name described his lumpy complexion.

"You'll get your chance at skateboarding too," Clark said.

Counselor Stacy Brunkhorst, in the Cherokee cabin, had her work cut out for her. She had two pugnacious black girls on her hands, Sateen Glasscock and Wysteria Brown, both of whom established their territory immediately.

Sateen shoved Paper Woman off her bunk onto the floor and proclaimed the bunk to be hers. Then Sateen looked over at Hazel Stanfield, who, like her brother, was trying to keep a low profile.

"The *sistuh* there got a better bed than you do, Wysteria," Sateen said, nodding toward Hazel.

"That's right," Wysteria said, nodding too. "What's your name, sistuh?"

"Hazel."

"Then I guess the bunk I'm takin' is Hazel's bunk." Hazel offered no resistance, quickly removing her things.

In the Iroquois cabin, Piano Legs's normally uncompetitive little boys were now joined by a small black boy named Joe Louis. He came into the cabin with clenched fists, looked around, and demanded, "Where's my bed?"

Piano Legs grabbed the rear of his pants and lifted him up with a solid snuggy.

"Ow! Hey! Whooo!" Joe flailed uselessly in the air.

"That's just to let you know who's boss around here," Piano Legs said, finally putting him down. Joe rubbed his rear. "Now then, I usually take a nap in here during the afternoon rest period, kid, and if you disturb me I'll give you a snuggy that'll put you right through the roof."

When Piano Legs left, Preston Wingo came over. "He's bad, Joe, better leave him alone."

"Well, I'm badder. I'm bad enough to fight any of you honkies. You wanna fight?"

The three boys shook their heads.

"Good," Joe said, looking truly relieved.

By dinnertime the camp was, rather than united, firmly divided into two hostile camps. As food was served, the original campers and the new ones silently sized each other up. One who didn't need to speak to establish his turf was the orphan George "Dogbreath" Mooney. When Curtis Kirk leaned toward him to ask innocently how he was, Dogbreath simply breathed. Curtis fled the room holding his mouth.

It was difficult for the original boy campers not to join the orphans in laughing.

Bad Henrietta Seeds plowed through her meal in a trice, then reached over to grab Dee Dee's plate and finish that off. Then she turned the other way and polished off Dianne's.

"You must really be hungry," June said wonderingly.

"Mmm."

"You certainly are nicely, um, developed," June added softly, her eyes wide.

"I had a baby," Bad Henrietta said, causing jaws around her to drop.

At the council ring, the orphans bunched together on the side opposite the old campers.

Steamboat paced back and forth in the center of the ring, giving his "teamwork, camp spirit, and fair play" talk. The old campers applauded, but the orphans remained stiffly silent.

Curtis, in buckskins and war paint, came out to do an Indian dance to the accompaniment of a cassette recording of jungle drums. Some of the older campers giggled as usual, but, oddly, the orphans were impressed at the show.

"You ever see such a jive act?" Luscious said loudly.

Then he pranced out to join Curtis with a few hot steps of his own, puffing out his chest and saying, "Whoo, whoo!"

Now the orphans applauded while the old campers sat silent.

Annie and Steamboat both sat watching closely. She leaned against him. "You think everything's okay?"

"Don't know. We'll let it ride for a while, let them get to know each other."

Just as Curtis was finishing his dance, Dogbreath Mooney dashed out and gave him a shot of breath, causing Curtis to stagger out of the circle.

Now everybody laughed.

Dee Dee, catching Bobby's eye, took the opportunity to slide over next to Charlie. Charlie, also catching Bobby's eye, took the opportunity to slide away, over next to Robin.

"I've decided not to speak to Dee Dee," Charlie said. "She's too shallow."

"Also because Bobby might beat you up again," she said, looking at him out of the corner of her eye.

"Heck no! I'm not scared of him."

"Then why are you sitting next to me?"

" 'Cause we have newspaper business to discuss."

"What business?"

"I forget."

As the council ring broke up, Vance saw Dianne coming toward him. He edged away quickly through the crowd.

Dee Dee punched Dianne lightly in the back. "Your *boyfriend* sure wanted to talk to you," she said, giggling.

"He just has lots on his mind."

"Sure, like how to avoid a thirteen-year-old dope."

"You wait!" Dianne stomped off toward her cabin, flipping her dark hair behind her.

That night some of the counselors gathered down at the lake. They were a worried bunch.

"What do you think's gonna happen?" Hulk asked. Vance shrugged.

"Things don't seem to be working out too smoothly," Stacy said.

"Too soon to tell," Vance said. "Lots of differences to get used to. It'll take time."

Hulk dug his toes into the sand and clasped his broad hands around his large knees. "I don't think we *got* too much time. Things are pretty hairy. I don't think we'll be seeing some of these little guys for much longer."

"Which little guys?" B.J. asked, punching him lightly in the shoulder.

"*Our* little guys. I mean, you know, the original ones. I think there's going to be some parents up here."

"Oh, I don't think so, Vance," Stacy said, leaning against him until she caught Hulk's brotherly stare and moved away. "Parents will understand. Most of them would rather be rid of their kids for a few weeks anyway, no matter what."

"Let's hope so. We can work it out, with a little time."

But Hulk's initial fears were correct. The next morning parents began to arrive. The parking lot was clogged with station wagons as parents hustled their offspring into the cars. Steamboat scurried around, fretting and trying to talk them out of it.

Harvey Allen cried his good-byes to Curtis, terribly disappointed that the greatest experience of his life was over. Neither of the Settlemire kids was happy to leave either. But Barbie Lipski was. She jumped joyfully into her car and rolled the windows up. Hazel and Thornton Stanfield were also relieved at going, as were their parents, who told Steamboat that the camp "no longer provides the kind of atmosphere we want our kids subjected to."

"What kind of atmosphere?" Steamboat asked

plaintively, holding out his hands. "I would think you'd welcome having more black kids here."

"Not that kind," Mr. Stanfield said huffily. "I do not want my son spending even two minutes of his life with a person called Doctor Death."

"Doctor Death? Who in blazes is—"

"Bye, Steamboat. Bye!" Furth Sklar and Clark Kent waved as they settled into their cars, looking the happiest they had since arriving at camp.

Saddest of all to leave was June Grabowsky. After a tough start, things had begun to look hopeful. Robin walked her to her car.

"Dee Dee and Dianne were just beginning to like me," June said sadly.

"Sure they were," Robin said, holding her hand. "You can write to them."

The orphans stood on the periphery of the hubbub, watching the exodus disdainfully.

"Hey, folks," Luscious called out, "we wasn't gonna *eat* them children!"

But whatever haste the parents had in claiming their children was encouraged by the event of Dogbreath Mooney's running out to lay a mouth blast on June Grabowsky's father just as he was settling behind the wheel. The man choked and frantically rolled up the window.

When the dust cleared, there were twenty of the original campers left, along with the twenty orphans. Steamboat and Annie stood together holding hands miserably as they watched the last station wagon clear the lot.

"Well, that's that," Steamboat mumbled.

"It's not so bad," Annie said, giving his hand a squeeze.

"Yeah, it's bad. All that money I'm gonna have to refund. We'll have to dip into the savings after all just to survive the season."

"We'll manage."

"Hey, that's right!" Steamboat suddenly brightened

and took her by the shoulders. "At least we've met Freddy's condition—we can pay the taxes. So we're over the hump!"

She smiled up at him and patted his big arm. "Right. Let's get back to work."

They strode into the camp grounds to lead the campers back to their activities. Both were smiling, and Steamboat was whistling. But notwithstanding their pleasant and confident manner, they both were apprehensive about the task that now lay before them.

The departure of thirteen of the original campers did more than just cut significantly into the number of paying customers at Camp Smilin' Through. It shook up severely all those who were left—campers, counselors, and the two camp directors alike. Some of those who had not left would actually have preferred to go, and most were worried about the rest of the season, now that the camp was composed of such a volatile mix of children.

There was now an even balance between original campers and new—twenty of each. And the old campers, already nervous with the arrival of the orphans and now no longer even the majority, were unsure of how to proceed. The orphans were certainly a new and challenging breed, and the original campers didn't know how to deal with them at all—whether to try to make friends with them, or avoid and ignore them, or to hide.

And even the orphans were nervous and subdued. For all those campers to leave because of *them* reaffirmed their feelings of frustration at not really belonging anywhere—not being wanted. For the orphans, being left or resented was not a new experience. But to be resented—even feared—on this scale, by so many all at once, was even more disturbing to them than were their usual experiences with desertion and hostility.

Added to that was the further unsettling fact that this time they were on completely unfamiliar turf.

For most of them, the closest they had been to a summer camp was to hear about it at school.

While there were certainly as many varieties of personality among the orphans as among the original campers, one effect of the desertion of so many campers was to impress both sides into more solid blocs. As with the old campers, not all the orphans were buddies. There was a pecking order similar to that among the old campers, and some orphans were even afraid of each other.

But still, the basic division asserted itself, and that was that half of them were orphans and half were not.

Had the new arrivals not been, each and every one of them, orphans, but simply poor or disadvantaged or different, the assimilation might have been easier, for both sides. But for the original campers, the very term "orphan" carried with it a dark and almost sinister meaning which they could barely comprehend.

For the orphans themselves, the same term seemed to mark them with an indelible stain which they could not erase—even though not to be an orphan was to most of them as inconceivable as to *be* one was inconceivable to the old campers.

So, at base the primary characteristic that sorrowfully divided the two groups was not really that the new children were unfamiliar to the camp, or that they were poor, or even that most of them were black. It was that they had no parents. In the minds and experience of the old campers, after all, it was parents who sent you to camp. To be an orphan was so fearsome a notion that they dared not contemplate it.

And the worst part of it was, the subject carried a taboo: nobody dared sit down and talk about it.

Nor were Steamboat and Annie free from fears and uncertainties about the new group and how the old group would deal with them. But they had to get on with camp, and so their manner in dealing with the problem was to get the activities back into full swing immediately.

Whatever else the orphans lacked in matters of traditional camp skills and spirit, they had, at least, a strong spirit of competitiveness and some particular skills to go with it—although of a style that often puzzled and dismayed the older campers and counselors alike.

At the morning swim session, some of the old campers made halfhearted attempts at kamikazes off the end of the docks. Some of the orphans refused to swim (several of them couldn't). A few waded into the water, but none would join in the kamikazes.

"Come on, you guys," Vance urged a bunch of boys clustered around Luscious Moncrief, "let's give it a try!"

"Ain't nothin' to try," Luscious muttered. "I know I ain't either a seagull or a stone."

Bobby Stenzel sauntered over. "Well, if you won't try kamikazes, maybe you got the guts for a swimming race against me—out to the raft."

"That don't take no guts."

"Let's do it then."

Luscious stomped behind him out onto the dock. The two boys dove off together and headed for the raft. Luscious had no real technique, but was powerful. Bobby had both technique and strength, and won by a couple of lengths.

"Swimming's for chumps," Luscious grumbled, hauling himself onto the raft.

"Oh, yeah?" Bobby flexed his muscles. "What's better?"

"Try me one-on-one in basketball."

"Yeah, basketball's all you guys can ever do."

Hulk climbed onto the raft just in time to separate the two before they came to blows.

Wysteria Brown, an angular twelve-year-old who commonly kept her eyes narrowed, sat on the beach holding spellbound the trio of little Cathy Shimizu, Paper Woman, and Robin Holt.

"See, at home what we do for fun is with pigeons. We get up on the bridge with 'em, over the street. Then we throw 'em down at the street. If you ain't got a strong enough arm, the pigeons just flap their wings and fly away 'fore they hit. But if you're good at it, grab that old bird right and throw it hard enough, that old pigeon just goes whack against the road and flies into a million pieces. Now, *that's* fun!"

The three girls stared at her with a mixture of fear and awe.

"Who wants to race me?" Bad Henrietta Seeds yelled as she muscled a canoe awkwardly into the water.

Several girls pushed Robin, the best canoeist, forward. Jane Smith lined them up and gave them the start signal. Henrietta thrashed and pummeled the water with her paddle, making pretty good headway by sheer force. But Robin won easily.

"You're much stronger that I am," Robin said as they rested side-by-side in the water, "and you'd be terrific at this if you just learned a few things. Want me to teach you?"

Bad Henrietta splashed her and paddled away, muttering, leaving Robin more confused than ever.

The boys were playing baseball—or seriously trying to. Bobby pitched for one side, Luscious for the other.

Bad Henry Seeds slid hard into second base, and Clark Brunkhorst tagged him even harder. They came up swinging. Harry Driscoll broke it up.

Bobby struck out Joe Louis, laughing as he did so. Little Joe strode immediately for the mound. Hulk trotted in to stand between them.

Luscious slammed a double, then tried to stretch it, barreling into Wolfman at third, knocking Wolfman's glove, hat, and the ball flying. They grabbed each other and spun each other around before the counselors broke it up.

"This isn't doing anybody any good," Hulk called finally. "Everybody find something else to do."

The game broke up and the players drifted off with a kind of weary resignation.

Among the counselors, only Curtis Kirk thought things were going well. In the girls' dining hall, his leaf-printing class was proceeding smoothly. A handful of the youngest girls and boys seemed to be enjoying themselves.

Two nine-year-old orphans—LaVerne Seeds (younger sister of Bad Henrietta and Bad Henry) and her best friend, Della Chesbro—at first thought the class was stupid. But Darlene Chavez, a delicately pretty and serious orphan of thirteen, thought it was beautiful, and so the younger orphans began to enjoy it as well.

The result was that when Curtis ended the class and returned to his cabin, his spirit was high and he felt euphoric.

But in the Navajo cabin he was confronted by three feisty little orphans who stood with arms folded belligerently.

"We two be the Soul Presidents," James Jefferson said proudly, nodding to James Monroe.

"Also known as the Two Bad Musketeers," said the sole white orphan, Dogbreath Mooney, gazing upon his two black cabin mates.

"Well, certainly none of *that* impresses me," Curtis sniffed.

"What does?" Jefferson asked.

"Oh, intellect and sensitivity, which perhaps you wouldn't know anything about."

"That so?" James Monroe watched while Jefferson slipped behind Curtis and got down on his hands and knees. "How's *this*?" Monroe gave Curtis a shove, tumbling him backwards over Jefferson.

As Curtis hit the floor, Dogbreath leaned over and gave him a mouth shot full in the face.

The three of them ran out, leaving Curtis coughing.

Gloria Kelly was a sullen and silent eleven-year-old orphan whose very presence in the Hopi cabin raised the hackles of Michelle Hinchman.

"What makes you tick, anyway?" Michelle asked gruffly, walking around the stony-faced black girl and looking her up and down. "What's the matter, cat got your tongue?"

Gloria eyed her calmly.

"Quit looking at me like that!" Michelle slapped her fists to her sides.

Joyce Cuccinello came cautiously over, holding her hands behind her as if afraid they might be soiled in the debate. "Maybe she just doesn't like to talk to strangers."

"Shut up! Hey, girl," Michelle continued to Gloria, "you know what happens to people who look at me like that? *This* is what happens!"

Whereupon she turned and butted Joyce in the stomach, sending the neat and proper girl toppling onto her precious dolls.

"What do you think of that!" Michelle rasped, standing face-to-face with Gloria.

Gloria just blinked and swallowed, remaining silent.

Joyce rubbed her stomach and tried to figure out just whose side she was supposed to be on.

In the Mohawk cabin, Paper Man and Turkey Wingo sat across from two black boys.

"My name is Julius Willigrod," said one of them, who was wearing dark sunglasses and had his hair done in corn-rows. "But I'm called Jet-Man. 'Cause I'm the fastest in my class and a wonder in the hun-nerd. Gonna win me an Olympic gold 'fore I'm old. Trust me, 'cause if I'm lyin' I'm dying'!"

He slapped palms with the other black boy, who was also wearing shades, but was bigger and stronger, looked meaner, and had a scar on his cheek.

"That's fine," Turkey said with a friendly smile. "Real fine."

"My name," the other boy said, "is not important. What I'm *called* is. In my neighborhood I'm known as Doctor Death."

Turkey blinked. "Why?"

"You don't be askin' Doctor Death *why*. You *learn* why, soon enough."

Paper Man gulped.

"But don't worry 'bout me none, right now," Doctor Death said, sprawling out on his cot. "I ain't gonna do nothin' while I'm here at this so-called camp."

"That's fine," Turkey said, sweating a little. "I think both of you are just fine."

"Bein' fine is our *line*," Jet-Man said, skinning palms again with Doctor Death.

Things weren't quite so smooth in the Choctaw cabin. Wolfman eyed Burrito-Face Rodriquez angrily, then launched himself at him, butting him heavily in the stomach.

Bad Henry Seeds burst through the door and, seeing Burrito-Face lying on the floor, started for Wolfman.

But Clark Brunkhorst came in right behind him and pulled them apart.

"Well, I ain't gonna fight two of you at once," Bad Henry said, spitting to the side.

"Nobody has to fight."

"That's the trouble with you folks," Bad Henry said scornfully. "You actually believe that."

It was not just the departure of the campers that depressed Steamboat, or even his precarious financial situation. He was also disturbed by his relationship with his son. He brooded about it through the morning and was annoyed by Annie's prodding him to brighten up.

But he knew he should talk to Chet, try somehow to bring them closer together. It was just that he always seemed to have so many other things on his mind lately. And anyway, he was Chet's father, after

all, and the relationship should just be there naturally.

But clearly it was not. He didn't really know how
to get things back on the right track.

The first thing, at least, was that he would have to
talk to him. But about what? He never seemed to be
able to say things just the way he wanted to, maybe
because he wasn't sure just what it was he wanted to
say.

He found himself wondering just what it was
other fathers and sons talked about. Oh, there was
school, of course, and sports, and dates—if they were
dating, which Chet was not yet involved with. In this
case, there was also camp to talk about, but that was
not a pleasant subject between them.

Somehow he felt there was something simple to be
said, something he couldn't quite put his finger on,
something that couldn't be misunderstood.

In any event, he wanted to talk to him. He caught
up with him on the way to lunch. "Hey, son, I just
wanted to say I'm sorry about yelling at you before,
in the—"

"Forget it, pop," Piano Legs said, moving away.
"Don't worry. I'm being a good little boy."

"But I wanted you to know I was sorry about it."

"It doesn't matter."

"It *does* matter!" Steamboat felt the familiar surge
of both anger and frustration that so often accom-
panied his attempts.

"Okay, it matters."

Trying to control himself, Steamboat let him go
ahead. He *was* sorry. But he was also offended. A son
shouldn't talk like that to his father. If one of his
other football players or counselors gave him such
snide comments he would boot him right out of the
place. They all knew that, but that wasn't what kept
them from mouthing off. What kept the others from
giving him lip was their feeling about him.

When so many other boys were fond of him and

respected him as a coach and camp director, Steamboat thought, why was his own son so different? Was Chet just a loser? Or was he, as his father, a loser? Was that why they couldn't relate warmly?

No. For Steamboat, there were no out-and-out losers. What he prided himself most on was that he took kids other adults couldn't handle and made them part of the team. Often he did that at the cost of winning football games, for example. But to get the kids to work together, to cooperate for a common goal, and have fun doing it, that was more important than winning. That was where the true victories lay.

But it was not more important than losing your son. Once the busy camp season was over, he thought, he would do something about it. The difficulty was that as soon as camp was over he would have to swing into preparation for football. Maybe after that . . .

Near dead silence filled the dining halls. Outside the boys' hall, Hulk and Vance stood with Stacy and B.J.

"You think we ought to pull Crazy Wilson Night on the orphans?" Stacy asked.

"No, no, *no!*" Vance said, slapping his forehead. "They'll kill us. They're liable to storm that house and *really* hang old Hulk!"

"Anyway," Hulk added soberly, "I don't want to go back to that house."

"Me neither," B.J. said.

"I guess it's unanimous," Vance said.

"The only thing that *is* around here," Stacy said.

After lunch, Steamboat and Annie went to their cabin. Steamboat paced back and forth in the living room.

"Stop worrying," Annie said as she puttered around straightening things up. "When Freddy gets here, you can just show him the balance sheet, prove we can pay the taxes, and that's that."

"That's not what's bothering me, Annie."

"What then?"

"Chet. Where did I go wrong?"

He did not often bring that subject up. While the subject disturbed her, she was pleased to have him raise it—it suggested maybe something would be done. "I won't deny that it sometimes breaks my heart to see you two being mean to each other," she said gently.

"You know what? I'm actually more confident that I can reach these orphans than I am about getting to Chet."

She looked at him pensively. "Maybe it's all part of the same thing. I mean, maybe they both have to be dealt with together."

"What do you mean?"

"You've been concerned with so *many* kids for so long, hundreds of kids over the years, with football and camp. Maybe you have to realize that Chet is not just another one of these hundreds of kids. Maybe he feels you just don't pay enough attention to *him*."

"I try to. I try to be nice to him."

"Yeah, but maybe he needs more than that. Sometimes I wonder if you realize that he's not just a little boy any longer, just somebody who tags along behind you. He's really more of an adult now, with needs and interests more independent from yours. Maybe he wants to be taken that way, by his father. Along with being nice."

"Possible." Steamboat stopped to stare out the window. "But maybe it's something deeper than that."

"Such as?"

"Annie." He turned to face her. "Could it be that he's just a bum? Or that I am?"

She snapped up straight. "Were any of the other kids you've dealt with successfully, even the most difficult ones, just bums? Or were you a bum in handling them?"

"No."

"They're here."

Steamboat swung around to the window to see Freddy Bolin and his sidekick Hal step from their car and head for the cottage.

Their welcome was cool and proper. Steamboat quickly spread out the ledger sheets in front of Freddy.

"There you go, Freddy, there are your blasted taxes!" He proudly traced his finger under a line of figures that showed enough money. "We got twenty new kids, just like that. That puts us over the hump."

"I see," Freddy said, scanning the figures and then glancing at Hal.

"So we're back in business!"

Freddy chuckled uncomfortably. "Well, unh, I see you can pay the taxes. But that's only part of it, as you know."

"Part of it?" Steamboat scratched his head.

"If you'll recall our conversation, I said you'd have to be able to pay the taxes *and* show me a reasonable profit—I think we said something about eight percent, didn't we, Hal?"

Hal nodded grimly.

"We need eight percent to make it worthwhile, of course. Otherwise we could just toss the money in a savings account and be better off. Right, Hal?" Hal nodded again. "Now, Steamboat." He looked up at him with a narrow grin. "I see where the taxes are taken care of, but darned if I can see a profit for me in here."

Steamboat, stunned for a few moments, now erupted. "Freddy Bolin," he barked, fists at his sides, "you're a darned dirty liar!"

"Hey—"

"You never said anything about profit!"

Freddy gave him a look of pained innocence. "Hal, did you hear me talk about profit?"

Hal nodded.

"Why you little ingrate, you dirty little bum—"

Hal stepped in front of him, cold-eyed and scowling.

Steamboat pushed him aside. "You never intended to let us keep the camp open, did you, Freddy? How can you call yourself your father's son, when you—"

"I acted in good faith, Steamboat," Freddy said, pushing the ledger sheets away.

"Good faith! You wouldn't know good faith if it raised your father from the grave! That's it! I'm through with you!" He seized Freddy roughly by the shoulders and spun him toward the door. "Get out of my house and out of my camp! You and your tough-guy friend! You both stink!"

Freddy held up a hand to Hal, who looked menacing, and smiled. "Gee, Steamboat, you don't offer me much choice about this camp. I'm afraid I'll have to sell—"

"Get out! And don't ever call me Steamboat again! Only my friends call me that! *Out!*"

They left quickly.

Steamboat slammed the door behind them, then stalked over to the sofa and smashed his powerful fist into a pillow. He was close to crying.

Annie came up behind him and put her arms around his waist. "We'll make it a wonderful last camp, old darling. What we're doing for all these orphans will make it a real special finale for all of us. And who knows? Maybe we can find another camp, build it up just like this one."

"I want to stay here, Annie," he said softly. "I want to keep Camp Smilin' Through. Actually"—he turned to face her, smiling thinly—"I'm tired of losing. I've been losing every fall on the football field. Now this. I don't want to lose here."

She watched his eyes, warm and damp. "You don't ever really lose, Steamboat, not really."

"Yeah, but I want to really *win* for once."

"I'm with you, whatever happens."

He studied her, pinching his lips together. Then he turned away. "Thanks, Annie."

During the rest period Turkey Wingo and Paper Man lay on their bunks staring at the ceiling of the Mohawk cabin. Doctor Death and Jet-Man played gin rummy with a dog-eared set of cards. Vance came wearily in and sagged onto his bunk.

"Hey, Vance," Turkey said, "how far is it to the sun?"

"Hunh?" Vance didn't open his eyes.

"I been thinking about, you know, the cosmos. How big everything is. How many different kinds of life there might be, far away from here, from this camp. And I wondered how far it is from here to the sun."

Vance sighed. "Ninety-three million miles—one of the few facts I know."

"How long would it take to get there in a car?"

Vance chuckled. "You're driving? Well, how fast is the car going, little buddy?"

"Oh, say ninety."

"Ninety, hunh? Well, let's see." Vance rolled over and picked up a pad and pencil from the table beside his bunk. "Just take a few minutes to figure it out."

Doctor Death slapped down his cards and looked over. "One million, thirty-three thousand, three hundred and thirty-three hours," he droned.

They all stared at him.

"Is that true, Vance?" Turkey asked incredulously.

"Well, it sounds like it's pretty close to—"

"It's exactly right, man," Doctor Death said.

They stared at him again for a few moments.

"How could you figure that out so fast?" Vance asked. "And in your head?"

Doctor Death shrugged and picked up his cards. "You learnin' about Doctor Death."

In the Cheyenne cabin, Della Chesbro and LaVerne

Seeds, inseparable friends, sat watching expressionlessly as Marian Pincu related her latest daily letter from her parents.

"My mommy said," Marian said in proud tones, "that when I get home we're going shopping and get me all my new school clothes. And listen to what my daddy says: 'We love you, punkin.' Now I'll open my package."

She ripped the wrapper off and pulled open the box of brownies. "Oh, goody!" She stuffed one in her mouth and chewed, rolling her eyes ecstatically.

Della and LaVerne looked at each other, then quickly moved over to sit on either side of Marian. Suddenly, together, they reached in and grabbed handfuls of brownies, shoving them into their mouths and chewing loudly.

"Hey, Kiki!" Marian howled to her counselor. "Look what they're doing!"

"Unh-hunh. You said you were going to share."

"But they didn't even *ask*! They just *took*!"

"Unh-hunh." Kiki's patience with any and all campers and camps was wearing thinner than ever. "Good idea." She snatched some brownies for herself while Marian watched teary-eyed.

In the Iroquois cabin, Preston Wingo lay reading *The Hardy Boys and the Tower Treasure.*

"You got another book?" little Joe Louis asked, looking down at him belligerently.

"Yeah, lots."

"Gimme one."

"What for? You don't wanna read books."

"Who says?"

"Well, I don't like to lend my books, especially since you probably haven't washed your—hey!"

Joe was already rummaging through Preston's locker. He found a book, *Gulliver's Travels,* pushed Preston back down on his bed, and flopped down in the corner to read. "Nothin' like a good book," he said, "to give a man *soul*."

Piano Legs paced around the cabin ignoring the conversation between the two boys. He was angry—anger was an emotion with which he was commonly afflicted after his father tried to talk nicely to him, yet an emotion he didn't really understand. Another thing he didn't really understand was that he had an almost desperate yearning not to be angry.

It confused him that the more he wanted to be close to his father, the more angered he became at his father's attempts to close the gap between them. But he didn't allow himself to think much about his yearnings—not ever.

Harry Driscoll leaned in the door. "What's happening?"

"Nothing," Piano Legs said. "What this camp needs is a little more spirit."

"Yeah."

They both grinned meanly and nodded.

They walked briskly over to Harry's Choctaw cabin and found Burrito-Face Rodriguez sitting alone, staring at the wall.

Joe Rodriguez, twelve, was a sallow, pudgy Chicano who always seemed to find himself on the low end of **the orphans' pecking or**der, a position his nickname seemed to affirm. He liked to be with other kids, as a matter of fact, especially girls. He combed his wavy black hair a lot, but nothing could be done to improve his pockmarked face. So he also spent a lot of time staring at walls.

Without speaking, Harry grabbed Burrito-Face by the arms while Piano Legs got him by the ankles. Swinging him between them, they lugged him at a trot into the lavatory where they gave him a quick, gurgling swirly.

Then they let him go, watching him run away, and waited in the shadows until Bad Henry Seeds walked in. They upended him and gave him a swirly.

"I'm gonna get you turkeys!" Bad Henry sputtered when they released him.

"Sure," Piano Legs said. "But first you better find yourself a towel. You're a mess."

In the Scarboroughs' back room, Charlie and Robin finished up the latest issue of the *Shoshone* and handed their work to Annie for typing.

They wandered outside. "You did a good job again," Charlie said.

"I like doing the paper with you."

Charlie blushed. "Come on"—he took her arm—"I have someplace I want to show you."

"Where?"

"Special place. It's quite a ways into the woods, but I know the way. We have lots of time. Come on."

"But where?"

"Just special. Come on, quick, before Annie's finished."

He grabbed her arm and they scampered into the woods.

Rest period for Dee Dee and Bad Henrietta Seeds was comprised of taunting Dianne about her plans and dreams for Vance.

"You're chicken, chicken, chicken!" Dee Dee said, dancing around and waggling her fingers.

"Yeah, you scared as a rabbit," Henrietta said.

"I'm *not*!" Dianne folded her arms and faced the wall.

"Okay. Do it *now*, then!" Dee Dee leaned toward her, taunting.

"Now?"

"Now!" said Bad Henrietta.

Dianne looked at them, her eyes widening. She stomped her foot. "All *right*, then! All right for you!"

They snuck into the woods and began working their way around through the underbrush that rimmed the lake.

When they reached the Mohawk cabin they could hear the boys in the distance on the ball field. They peeked in through the screen to see Vance alone, asleep on his bunk.

"Maybe now wouldn't be a good time," Dianne whispered, "since he's asleep."

"He's *alone!*" Dee Dee hissed between giggles. "Do it now!"

They pushed her around to the door and shoved her inside.

Vance sat up with a start. "What? Who? What's going on?" He rubbed his eyes.

"Um, unh—" Dianne looked nervously around.

Vance took a deep breath and peered at her. "You want something?"

"Unh, er, um—"

"I see." He stared at her closely. "You, unh, wanted to see me alone."

"Well, unh, that is, yes, I guess."

He heard the low giggling from outside. "I see. This is your big chance, hunh?"

"Unh, um—"

"Okay." Suddenly he sprang off the bunk and came toward her, smiling devilishly, holding his arms out. "You want to kiss me?"

"Oh! Unh—" She backed away.

"Yes! Let's kiss! Then we'll be engaged! Then we'll get married! Then we'll raise a family! Let's kiss, Dianne!"

She gave a little squeak, then bolted for the door. He caught her, spun her around, and backed her outside. "Hold it, girls!"

Dee Dee and Henrietta, about to run, froze.

"This little experiment in romance is over!" Vance shoved Dianne toward them. "If you don't get back to your side of the camp, I'm gonna sic the little boys on you and make leaf prints on your rears! Now *move it!*"

They tore off around the lake.

Vance turned to see Hulk leaning against the cabin, holding his sides from silent laughter. "What's it to you?" Vance snapped angrily.

"Oh, nothing, my prince. You're quite the Romeo."

"At least they finally got it out of their system," Vance muttered, stalking into the cabin.

The two girls flanked Dianne as they ran toward their cabin.

"How's your *husband*?" Dee Dee sang.

Suddenly Dianne leaped at her and grabbed her around the throat with a hammerlock. "If you ever mention it again, I'll break your neck!"

Dee Dee struggled for breath, tearing at Dianne's arm.

Dianne released her, and they stood looking at each other, breathing heavily.

"Now," Dianne said, "you say cross my heart and hope to die, stick a needle in my eye, I'll never mention Vance Brehm to my best friend Dianne Wingo again! Say it! Or I'll mess up that pretty face of yours right here and now!"

Dee Dee, petrified by this unfamiliar rage and strength in Dianne, quickly agreed, promising as ordered.

"Well," said Henrietta as the three resumed walking, "at least we had some fun."

Charlie and Robin were deep in the woods. Robin began to shiver.

"Are you sure we won't get lost, Charlie?"

"Naw, I come here all the time."

"Aren't you scared—you know—of Crazy Wilson?"

"Naw. You don't believe all that old stuff, do you? There isn't any Crazy Wilson."

"I don't know . . ."

They reached the entrance to a cave nearby hidden by brush and boulders.

"Don't be afraid," he said. "There's nothing in there. It doesn't even go very far." He stooped and crawled a few feet inside. "See?" He waved to his blanket and pile of books. "This is where I come to read. I used to use that old culvert, but then Preston Wingo started following me there. So I found this place. Nobody knows about it."

She looked around. "Sure is quiet out here," she said in a quaking voice.

"Yeah, but it's really great. Come on, sit on my blanket."

She crawled in hesitantly and sat beside him. "Have you been all the way in the cave, to the end?"

"Well, almost."

"Everybody says Crazy Wilson was ugly as sin and killed his whole family." She looked into the blackness deeper in the cave.

"Naw, they'd have caught any guy who did that."

"What would you do if you ran into him?" She looked at him fearfully.

"Aw, I'd just say, 'Don't mess with me, Crazy Wilson, or I'll sic my girlfriend on you!' " He blushed and looked away.

"Am I your girlfriend?" Her voice was soft, and she blushed too.

"Well, sort of, if you—"

Suddenly a low howl came from deeper in the cave, a wolflike moan. They stiffened.

The howl came again.

"The Hound of Death!" Charlie gasped.

They grabbed each other, shaking with terror.

Robin screamed.

Standing over them, looking down at them, was an old wrinkled Indian wearing tattered buckskins and a black stocking cap.

CHAPTER
7

"I'm Crazy Wilson."

They gaped up at him, trembling beyond control.

Then the old Indian cracked a wide smile. "Yup, that's me." He tapped his chest with a gnarled thumb. He cocked his head and pursed his lips and looked down at them thoughtfully. "Can I offer you two scared bunnies a mug of hot chocolate?"

They blinked and gulped and looked at each other. Charlie managed to nod.

"Custer!" The Indian looked off into the cave. "Here, boy!"

Out ambled a shaggy old mutt, gray-black hair matted over his back and around his muzzle, happily wagging his stumpy tail. The dog went directly up to Charlie and Robin and licked their faces.

"Yes sir, there's your Hound of Death," Crazy Wilson said, chuckling raucously. "Come on into my cave."

He waggled a bent finger at them and they followed, stooping through the darkness.

Then they emerged into a candle-lit chamber furnished with a ratty old sofa and a couple of patched-together wooden chairs.

"Yup. Here it is, where I spend most of my time. Nobody bothers me here."

They looked around, and at him, with nervous wonder.

"Sit, sit." He waved them to the sofa and put a pot of milk over a flame. "This here's fresh, stole it just this morning from an old farmer that don't treat his cows right." He chuckled. "Yup, whenever your camp there goes on its Crazy Wilson expeditions, I always love to watch. But this year I gave it a little twist. Went upstairs in my old house and haunted it real-like. Scared your counselors half silly, I suspect." He laughed grandly, deepening the crevices in his brown skin.

He served them their hot chocolate and stood smiling down at them. "Now, what do you think of all that?"

"I . . . I don't know," Charlie sputtered, clearing his throat and glancing at Robin. "It's so strange, seeing you."

"Yeah, I imagine so." He drew a rough hand back and forth across his nose. "But it's tough being a legend all the time. I sometimes hanker for company, but mainly I keep to myself because I don't want anybody disturbing my peace and quiet with a whole lot of questions. Nobody but you two even knows I live here in this cave."

Charlie cleared his throat again, beginning to relax a little. "I don't think anybody even knows you really *exist*."

"Oh, they know, they know, some of 'em. They know I don't bother nobody—except maybe a few of these farmers around here who let everything go to waste. I mainly just hunt and fish for food, grow some vegetables here and there in the woods, and generally live like, well, like an Indian, I guess you might say."

"Are you really an Indian?" Robin asked, sipping her chocolate.

"Not only an Indian, I'm a *chief*. Last of the Chumash tribe of the Iroquois Nation. Yup. Regular chief. Trouble is, I'm a chief that's got no Indians!" He laughed loud and long, bending backwards, his raspy voice echoing through the chamber. "Wanna see?"

He went over to the wall and pulled up an oilskin cloth to reveal a fine buckskin outfit with silver, beads, and fringe, along with a magnificent eagle feather headdress.

"Put it on!" Charlie begged. "Please?" His eyes glowed, as did Robin's, at the sight.

"Only for special occasions. And there hasn't been one since I can remember." He replaced the oilskin and rubbed his hands together. "Well, I guess it's time for you to get back to camp. They'll be missing you. Come and see me again."

They handed him their empty cups and nodded.

"We'd like to, very much," Charlie said.

"But one thing."

They blinked at him.

"I must swear you to secrecy about this, about me, about all you've seen here."

"Yes," Charlie said, "we promise."

"Or else," he gave them a crooked grin, "my ghost might *get you!*"

He laughed his coarse laugh and waved good-bye.

They left and headed back through the woods, dazed and speechless.

Jet-Man Willigrod couldn't stand it any longer. He had been watching with a bunch of other orphans as the old campers practiced kamikazes off the dock. Finally, when Bobby Stenzel soared and splatted to what he called "the best of the best," Jet-Man could stand it no more.

"All *right!*" he shouted. "Clear the dock!" He trotted up a hundred feet from the dock, crouched into a sprinter's start position, and took off.

He came like a blur, propelling himself high off the end of the dock, arms and legs spread wide, wailing "Whoooo!" and belly whopped into the water in explosive fashion—five feet farther out than anybody else. He came up sputtering and coughing and holding his belly, but with a clenched fist raised in the air.

"All *right!*" Vance yelled, waving his fists. "Now *that's* what I call a *kamikaze!*"

"Look out!" Now came Bad Henry, not as fast as Jet-Man but still flying out over the dock and over the water to land with a smack almost as far out as Jet-Man.

For a few moments the old campers were too surprised to react. But then Clark Brunkhorst took off on a new try, screeching as he flung himself off the dock, arms and legs flailing. He landed in the general area of Jet-Man.

So the competition was on in earnest. They all lined up for tries. Bad Henry elbowed into line again ahead of Wolfman.

"No you don't!" Wolfman growled. He butted Bad Henry in the stomach. Harry and Hulk jumped between them.

None of this was lost on the girls' side. Michelle Hinchman did a wild, bellowing kamikaze, and came up taunting the orphan girls. "None of you can do it! You can't even swim!"

That prodded Sateen Glasscock in line. Sateen was a strong girl of twelve, one of the few orphans who actually knew what it was like to have parents. Hers had been killed in an auto accident two years before, and she had since been shunted among various foster homes, ending up in the county juvenile center. She carried herself now with a belligerence that alienated her from the others in her cabin—even the other orphan, Wysteria Brown.

Sateen tolerated no slurs. So she stepped angrily into line, knocking down cabin mate Paper Woman, who got up crying.

Sateen took off running for the dock, but Michelle tripped her, sending her sprawling. Michelle dove on top of her and the two wrestled until Jane and Stacy broke it up.

B.J. helped Paper Woman to her feet. "Next time," B.J. said, wiping the tears off the snuffling girl's cheeks, "punch her back."

"I'm scared to," sniffed Paper Woman. "And I don't want to fight anybody."

"That's not fighting, really, that's just taking care of number one."

For the boys, the competition moved on to skateboarding, and Bad Henry was the first orphan to try it. He fell off the first couple of times, ignoring the laughs and jeers from the fans of Clark Brunkhorst, but refused to get off the track until he had made it down all the way to the dock without falling.

The jeers gave way to reluctant praise for his brave persistence. Finally he made it down and held his fists high.

"Not bad for a beginner," Clark said quietly to Turkey, "but he'll never catch up to me."

Other orphans moved in to try, alternating with old campers. But the competitive spirit was not shared joyfully as it had been before the orphans arrived, and the activity soon palled for everybody.

Campers left their swimming, skateboarding, ball playing, and other pursuits and drifted into their cabins.

But even in the cabins the tension was unrelieved. In the Cheyenne cabin, Marian Pincu opened her daily box of brownies, all the while nattering about how her parents were taking a vacation in Las Vegas.

Della and LaVerne snatched the brownies from her once again and gobbled them up, sending Marian scampering over to complain tearfully to Kiki.

"Oh, shut up," Kiki said, pushing her away. "I'm reading." She hadn't been, but now she picked up a magazine and began thumbing through it.

A Go Fish game was going on in the Penobscot cabin, the three orphan girls seeming to team up against the three old campers. Jane Smith came in and interrupted the game to spread some women's lib pamphlets on the table.

"What's all this garbage?" asked Jackie Lee Sutcliffe, a round-faced girl with shiny straightened hair.

"This is the stuff you should be thinking about," Jane said, smiling at her and the others, "about women's power."

"Women's power! Phoo! Ain't nothin' about us *sisters* in here!" She shoved the pamphlets away.

"Well, we're all sisters, under the skin. We all have to strive for women's rights."

"Double phoo. I got enough trouble just dealin' with my *skin*, without goin' underneath to help no more causes."

"Well," Jane persisted, steadfastly pleasant, "we all have to work at things together, black and white, all sisters."

Tina Rodriguez, Burrito-Face's sister and a fiercely competitive Chicano whose ambition was to become a lawyer for the main purpose of putting Anglos away in the slammer, bounced up clenching her fists. "You get off my back about us all being sisters, Miss Smith! You got something to say about Chicano power, I'll listen."

Jane carefully gathered up the pamphlets. "I'm sorry. I don't know much about that."

"I'll buy that!" Tina huffed, nodding at all of them.

"But maybe you could help me learn, tell me about Chicanos."

"If you don't know nothin' by now, I ain't gonna be the one to fill you in."

"Okay." Jane determined to learn more about Chicanos, and blacks as well, especially the women. It seemed that she knew less and less every day.

As usual, the morning handicraft classes seemed the only oasis in the desert of hostilities. Robin was stitching a wallet under the supervision of Gerri Belardi. Darlene Chavez came in shyly, her hands behind her back. Then she held out a leaf print she had made in Curtis Kirk's class and handed it to Robin.

Before Robin could respond, Darlene ran out.

But such friendly overtures were rare throughout the camp. At lunch Michelle was sitting next to the ever-silent Gloria Kelly and jabbering to whoever would listen about her love of football and how she planned to try out for the boys' team at school in the fall. "I'm not gonna be just some smart-haired Farrah Fawcett-Majors scared to play anything rough," she said.

Suddenly Gloria stiffened and glared at her.

"All Farrah's worried about is protecting those nine hundred teeth she flashes all the time," Michelle went on.

"Farrah Fawcett-Majors is beautiful, you chump!"

Everyone stopped eating to look at Gloria, who had spoken her first words since entering camp.

Recovering quickly from her surprise, Michelle sneered at her. "So, you can actually speak! Well, listen here, chump. Farrah Fawcett-Majors is a skinny chump, just like you!"

The two girls lunged at each other, tumbling off the bench. B.J. pried them apart. "That's enough! Now, Michelle, I guess you deserve some kind of congratulations for opening up a new line of communications around here. Gloria, I'm glad you're willing to speak up for yourself. So at least we can talk to each other. From now on, let's restrict ourselves to talking!"

In the afternoon, Curtis was alone in the handicraft room, experimenting with leaf prints. James Jefferson and James Monroe, the self-proclaimed Soul Presidents, ambled in, followed closely by Dogbreath Mooney.

"Well, if it isn't the Soul Presidents," Curtis said, continuing his work.

"Can you make prints of other things besides leafs?" James Monroe asked.

"Of course. Interested in learning?" He looked up hopefully.

"Sure, why not."

They watched him for a while as he dipped leaves in the tray of poster paint.

Then, nodding as a signal, James Jefferson leaped on Curtis's back while the other two grabbed him around the neck and forced his face down into the paint. Then they yanked his face over to the print paper and pressed it down hard, rolling it back and forth like a thumb making a fingerprint.

The result was a somewhat smashed but recognizable face print of Curtis Kirk.

Dogbreath gave him a breath shot and the three left, linked arm in arm, laughing merrily.

In the Iroquois cabin, Alan Friedman, Hayden Peake, and Preston Wingo—joined by the only orphan in the cabin, little Joe Louis—made a plan. They considered its ins and outs, chances and dangers. Finally they decided it was worth it.

They waited patiently and silently while Piano Legs came in, stretched, yawned, and flopped down on his bunk to take his customary afternoon nap.

When he was snoring loudly, Joe silently pulled some pieces of clothesline from his pants pocket, and the boys leaped on Piano Legs.

He woke up dazed, wrestling to try to clear his head and fend them off. But the boys worked quickly and efficiently, rather desperately, in fact, so scared were they of failing. In moments they had him tied hand and foot. Joe then stuffed an old sock into his mouth as a gag.

Struggling with his weight and squirming, the boys hauled him outside. They loaded him onto a small cart and rolled him quickly over to the lavatory and inside. They yanked him off the cart and, employing all sets of hands, shoved his head down into the toilet bowl to give him one of the more monumental swirlies.

They were interrupted—too late—by Hulk. "Hey, what in blazes is going on?"

Having succeeded, they fled. Hulk untied and ungagged Piano Legs.

"I'll get them rotten little—"

"No you won't, Piano Legs. You got what you deserved."

"But, but—"

"Shut up and forget it, or I'll give you a personal ten-minute swirly that'll truly make your head swim."

"But, but—"

"Listen." Hulk shoved him down onto a bench in the corner. "I don't know what's bugging you, but it's not the fault of these kids. You better figure out what it is and work it out."

Piano Legs slumped and stared at the floor.

"Listen, friend—and I *am* your friend, believe it or not—everybody here would just as soon like you as not like you. So quit bringing all this garbage on yourself. You got a problem, you deal with that directly. And your problem ain't these kids. Okay?"

Piano Legs sat silently as Hulk tossed the pieces of rope into his lap and left.

After dinner, Charlie and Robin snuck out of camp and ran through the woods to Crazy Wilson's cave. They presented him with gifts they had made—Robin her wallet and Charlie a leaf-printed coffee mug.

"Gosh," was all Crazy Wilson could say as he looked admiringly at their handiwork.

"Can we smoke a peace pipe with you?" Charlie asked.

"Don't have one." Charlie shook his head sadly. "Wish I did. All I got is a fine Cuban cigar. My father gave it to me before he died. Where he got it, I don't know. But, well, maybe now's as good a time as any. That'll be our peace pipe."

He dug it out from his pile of prized possessions, lit it, and passed it to them. Charlie and Robin took the briefest of puffs, coughed, and handed it back for him to finish.

He leaned back on the sofa, smoke curling around his head, and stared at the ceiling. He lapsed into a reverie, telling them how the huge boulder had somehow become dislodged from the hillside after a heavy rain and rolled down and crushed his family— all while he had been out in the woods hunting with Custer. Tears came to his eyes. "I don't know how it happened. They was what I was living for. Now the story goes that I did it. Folks that know me know I didn't do it, of course. But I guess it's part of the legend. Wish it wasn't. Wish it wasn't part of the legend *or* the truth, what happened . . ."

His voice trailed off, and Robin and Charlie put their arms around him.

It was the day of another dance night. Camp activities went on as usual, albeit with a decreasing enthusiasm. The orphans joined in more readily, but a kind of cloud hung over everything. Campers began counting down the few days left.

Steamboat seemed to them detached in a way, preoccupied with something, distant in a way they hadn't seen before.

Things moved along in a kind of dull routine, a sort of uneasy truce.

Marian Pincu moped in her cabin. She hadn't had a letter or a box of goodies from her parents in three days. "Why haven't I heard from them?" she whined to Kiki.

"Who knows? They haven't had time."

"But they *always* have time. They love me more than anything." She turned to Della and LaVerne, who were watching sullenly. "They'll do anything for me. Why, just last spring they—"

"They're dead," LaVerne said.

Marian gasped.

"Yeah," Della chimed in, "they're dead, all right."

"They're *not!*" Tears rolled down Marian's cheeks. "They're in Las Vegas!"

"Probably a car accident," LaVerne said calmly, "just like with Sateen's folks."

"No, no—" Marian choked on her tears.

"Too bad, Pincu," Della went on, shaking her head dolefully, "now you're an orphan too. I guess you won't go braggin' no more about havin' folks. You're gonna have to come and live with us in foster homes and get kicked out and sent back and probably end up in reform school."

"You out of luck, child," LaVerne said.

"No, no!" Marian threw herself at Kiki. "They're not dead, are they?" She tried to bury her face in Kiki's shoulder. "Are they?"

Kiki gently pushed her off. "Who knows? Everybody knock it off. We got a dance tonight. Think about that."

Marian sunk onto her knees in a corner, crying softly. LaVerne and Della watched her, showing no emotion at all.

In the Cherokee cabin, Sateen Glasscock was doing her hair, teasing out her broad Afro.

Paper Woman watched with deep curiosity this strange procedure. "Can I touch it?"

"Hunh? Touch what?"

"Your hair. It's so, well, unusual."

"Hey, chump," Sateen said, making a fists, "I'm gonna bust your skinny nose."

"I didn't mean anything by it. It's just that you look so—"

Sateen shoved her harshly, sending her stumbling to her knees. Then she pushed her over backwards and sat on her stomach and started yanking her blond hair.

"Don't do that!" Paper Woman screeched. "I don't like pulling my hair!"

"Get used to it, chump!" Sateen gave her hair a severe yank. "I'm gonna teach you something about hair!"

"No!" Suddenly Paper Woman lashed out furiously. She hit and kicked and bit Sateen with more strength and passion than even she would have believed possible.

Sateen slid off her, but Paper Woman intensified her attack, leaping at her and belting her with hard slaps to both sides of the face. "Don't you ever pull my hair again or I'll . . . I'll—"

Abruptly she ceased her onslaught and stomped out of the cabin, leaving Sateen crumpled on the floor.

Stacy rushed in. "What happened, Sateen?" She knelt over the girl, who got slowly up.

"Nothin'!" She began to sob.

"Tell me what happened."

"I ain't a bad girl, Stacy," she sobbed, collapsing into Stacy's arms. "I didn't mean to make Paper Woman so mad."

"I know, I know. But you've been pretty mean to her sometimes."

"I know that." Her chest heaved. "I didn't want to be. But I don't want to be no orphan! I loved my folks! I want them back! I wish I was dead, like them!" She wailed out of control as Stacy tried to comfort her, rocking her back and forth in her arms.

"I know, honey, I know. It'll be all right . . ."

Outside, Paper Woman too broke down and sobbed.

Steamboat was not in camp. He was in town, standing before an officer of the bank who was shaking his head somberly.

"There's just no way, Mr. Scarborough. You can't borrow on a camp you don't own, and you have nothing else for us to base a loan on. I appreciate what you're trying to do, but we just can't risk it. I'm sorry."

Steamboat nodded, took a deep breath, and left.

It was painful for him to enter his savings bank, where he and Annie had so faithfully deposited money over the years for Chet's college education. He took out his passbook and filled out a withdrawal slip and went up to the teller's window.

"May I help you, sir?" asked the smiling young man.

"Unh"—Steamboat closed his eyes and crumpled up the withdrawal slip—"no, thanks."

Annie was waiting for him in their camp cottage when he got back, his shoulders sagging with disappointment. "It's okay," she said, taking his arm.

He pulled away. "There's just no hope, Annie. We're going to lose the camp."

"Maybe we'll think of something."

"What? More Martians maybe?" He sighed. "Maybe Freddy'll let us have a condominium at wholesale, for old times' sake," he said bitterly.

She tried to pat his hand. "Come on, cheer up. It's not like you to quit."

He pushed her hand away. "Quit telling me to cheer up! The camp's finished. Camp Smilin' Through is washed up—dead!"

In the back room, where everything could be heard, Charlie pulled the green eyeshade off his head. He and Robin looked at each other, stunned.

The after-dinner council ring went on as usual, Steamboat gathering everybody together cheerfully as if nothing had happened. Hulk stepped before the fire to present the premier award of the day, a special gold brick to Alan, Hayden, Preston, and Joe Louis for, as he said, "unspecified service to humanity."

As a cheer spread over the group, Piano Legs blushed and looked at the dirt.

Sateen slid over to Paper Woman. "I'm sorry I was bad to you," she whispered.

"Oh, that's okay. Sorry I hurt you."

"Aw, you didn't hurt me, really."

"Good, I'm glad."

"I don't want to fight nobody no more," Sateen said.

"Me neither."

The two girls let their shoulders touch, then looked shyly away.

Vance stepped to the center of the ring. "There were only a few fair kamikazes the last few days, campers. I need to see a *great* kamikaze or camp can't end! I'll keep you all here till the snow flies, unless we get a kamikaze to beat the world!"

Cheers went up, mixed with groans.

Then Annie took his place before the fire. "Kids, you know there's a dance tonight. I want you all to behave yourselves. Young ladies and gentlemen is what I want to see."

Some of the boys groaned.

"You know what I mean," she continued, silencing them. "You can still have plenty of fun."

Harry leaned over to Piano Legs. "Let's give out a few complimentary swirlies before the dance, just to clean a few brats up."

"Naw," Piano Legs said, looking away. "I'm too tired." He glanced over at his father, and for a moment the two pairs of eyes locked. When Steamboat smiled, Piano Legs looked away.

"Guess you won't be dancing with Vance tonight," Dee Dee whispered to Dianne.

"Nope. Maybe you'd like to have a try."

"Nope."

They giggled together.

Now, across the lake, torches appeared, very low against the water and small in the distance. Hulk began to read aloud some material Curtis had given him about the Indian war ceremony they were about to witness. While he droned on about the symbolism of the ceremony and the torches wiggled in the distant air, the kids continued to buzz about this and that.

Vance sat next to Doctor Death. "Well, just a couple more days of camp."

"Yeah. Exactly two thousand, five hundred minutes. Or one hundred fifty-one thousand, two hundred seconds."

"Wow. Where'd you learn to do math like that in your head?"

"I didn't. I just do it."

"You ever study math?"

"Never study nothin'."

"Well, you've got *some* talent."

"That's why I'm called what I'm called."

"Doctor Death? Why?"

" 'Cause death is when the counting stops. And I count everything up to then."

On the other side of the circle, Burrito-Face Rodriguez arrived, his hair slicked down, his face shiny clean. He edged shyly up to Paper Lady. "I'm gonna dance with you tonight!" he blurted out. Then, leaving her amazed, he darted off into the night.

Now, across the lake, the smooth shape of the war canoe could be discerned in the dim, dramatic light of the torches it carried. Hulk continued his narration as the attention of the campers was drawn ever more surely to the sight of the splendid canoe approaching across the water.

But then, oddly, as the canoe was about a hundred feet from shore, it began riding lower and lower in the water. The boys paddling it struggled harder and harder. Finally after another fifty feet, the prow disappeared completely under the water and the boys were rowing nothing, just splashing waist-deep in the lake. The torches floated beside them for a few seconds, then sputtered and sank.

Bobby Stenzel and Turkey Wingo were convulsed with laughter, slapping each other on the back.

Vance ran out to rescue Hayden Peake, who kept screaming that he couldn't swim. Curtis slogged in through the water, his buckskins weighing him down, his headdress feathers floating away. He was beside himself, nearly speechless. He waved his soggy buckskin arms pathetically.

Finally he could speak. He could yell. "I'll kill whoever did this!"

"I guess we're dead then," Bobby said to Turkey, holding his sides from laughter-induced pain.

"It was worth it. I knew those fake patches would let loose!"

It took a long time for Curtis to calm down, and for everybody to get over the unexpected debacle. But the dance was coming up in an hour, so at last everybody headed for their cabins for final primping.

The dance began smoothly enough. Bobby and Dee Dee took center stage in the boys' dining hall to do a fairly slick hustle, while around them others engaged in various energetic versions of the hustle, the frug, and the twist.

Gradually the orphans moved out onto the floor, and the real dancing began. Doctor Death and Wysteria Brown led the way, causing heads to turn with some real Soul Train routines. Della Chesbro and James Monroe joined them, stomping and whirling and kicking their legs out.

No sooner did the old campers try to copy their uptown moves than Luscious Moncrief and Bad Henrietta Seeds pounced onto the floor doing a particularly dazzling old-fashioned lindy hop. They waggled and pirouetted, and Luscious swung Henrietta up over his shoulders and down between his legs, never missing a beat.

The orphans were clearly taking over with their superior skills and experience in the coolest of the dances.

Then Bobby grabbed Dee Dee's arm again and hauled her out among the flashy orphans. They aped the orphans' moves well and rallied other old campers behind them.

The floor was rocking with heavy beats and stomping feet; it was the liveliest and happiest scene yet at camp. The orphans were proudly asserting themselves, and the older campers were losing their inhibitions and swinging freely.

Then Burrito-Face Rodriguez, his hair newly slicked down with grease and the roughest bumps on his face smoothed with talcum, asked Paper Woman to dance.

"No, thanks," she said, not looking at him.

"Why not?" he asked gruffly.

"I just don't want to."

"You were dancing before."

"I don't want to anymore."

"Hey girl!" Abruptly he grabbed her roughly by the arm. "I love you!"

"Arrrg!" She pulled away.

Burrito-Face turned sullen. He growled and snarled. He stalked onto the floor and tripped Charlie, who stumbled against Robin.

"Hey, watch what you're doing!" Charlie snapped, recovering his balance.

"Watch yourself, snot-nose!"

Several dancers stopped to look on.

"*You* watch!" Charlie gave him a shove.

Burrito-Face took a wild swing, which missed.

Quickly Vance stepped between them.

But other pushing and shoving had started. Luscious and Bobby bumped shoulders, then grabbed each other's shirts and wrestled to the floor.

Jet-Man did a quick Muhammad Ali shuffle step and jabbed Turkey Wingo in the midsection. They squared off like boxers.

Michelle Hinchman spun Wysteria Brown around and butted her in the stomach, drawing a loud "Ooof!" from the surprised girl.

Then Wolfman tapped Doctor Death on the shoulder, causing him to turn around, whereupon Wolfman butted him in the chest, toppling him over backward.

Counselors scurried frantically back and forth trying to break up the fights. Vance kept a hold on Charlie and Burrito-Face, while he tried to get in front of Michelle, who waggled her potent head back and forth like an angry bull. Harry Driscoll managed to get between Jet-Man and Turkey and keep them at arms' length.

But right in front of Harry, Bad Henry Seeds and Clark Brunkhorst were glaring daggers at each other, clenching their fists threateningly.

"All right, you jerks," Harry said, eying first Bad Henry then Clark, "you might as well get it outta your systems. What are you waiting for?"

"Nothin'!" Bad Henry took a roundhouse swing at Clark, the punch thudding into Clark's shoulder.

Then Clark swung. It was a solid right that smacked into the side of Bad Henry's head, dropping him.

Bad Henry's head hit a bench as he went down. He lay still.

Everything stopped as everybody stared down at Bad Henry.

"What happened?" Clark asked, dazed by his own action.

Steamboat knelt over the still form of Bad Henry. He pulled his eyelids back and felt for pulse along his neck. A trickle of blood came down over Bad Henry's ear.

"Annie!" Steamboat shouted. "Let's get him to the hospital!"

"What happened? What *happened*?" Clark cried, holding out his arms to the crowd packed around Bad Henry.

Steamboat and Vance and Hulk cradled the unconscious boy in their arms, carried him out, loaded him into the station wagon, and headed for the hospital.

"What happened?" Clark asked weakly as the crowd filed out of the dining hall in shocked quiet.

* * *

Steamboat paced back and forth in the waiting room off the main corridor, shaking his head from time to time and muttering under his breath.

Annie sat silently, wringing her hands together.

Finally a doctor came in, and Steamboat and Annie stepped up to him instantly, questioning with their eyes.

"We don't know anything yet," the doctor said softly. "We're doing a brain scan. He could snap right out of this, or we could have to go into his brain to relieve pressure—if that's what's causing it. We just don't know." He patted each of them on the shoulder and retreated back down the corridor.

Steamboat resumed his pacing while Annie stared out the window.

Gerri Belardi and Bad Henrietta Seeds walked softly into the waiting room.

"We came in the truck," Gerri said to Steamboat. "I hope that's all right."

"Of course. I'm terribly sorry about what's happened, Henrietta. I hope we can—"

"We wanted to come to camp," Henrietta said with difficulty, fighting back her tears, "really *wanted* to. We wanted to have a good time. But everything went wrong."

"I know. Sometimes it seems that way. We're all so—"

"And now my brother's going to die."

"No, he isn't," Annie said urgently, coming over to her. "He'll be all right."

Henrietta held back the tears no longer. She wept openly but silently. Annie put an arm around her, but Henrietta spun angrily away and went across to the corner, where she leaned her face against the wall so that nobody could see her angry tears.

Back at the camp, everyone remained in a state of near shock at the sudden turn of events. Clark Brunkhorst sat disconsolately in his cabin, eyes closed, from time to time shaking his head and grinding his teeth. Harry patted him on the shoulder. So did Piano Legs.

Luscious Moncrief stuck his head in the door. "Nothin' bad better happen to the brother," he said with cool rage.

"I tried to fight him fair!" Clark blurted, his eyes sad and pleading.

"Ain't nothin' fair about a brother lyin' in the hospital."

"Get out of here, Luscious," Harry commanded.

"Just remember," Luscious said, nodding before he turned and plodded off.

Clark started after him. "Gotta explain . . ."

"No." Harry stopped him with a hand on his shoulder. "The fight was my fault. I could have stopped it and I didn't. I guess I just wanted to see you teach him a lesson. I was stupid. It's not your fault."

"I didn't mean to hurt him."

"No. But he's in the hospital now."

"You think he might be all right, hunh?" It was a fearful question.

"Let's go to the hospital."

"You think we should, Harry?"

"I don't particularly like Bad Henry, I admit. But then, I have a hard time liking anybody. And I think if a guy's hurt bad, he ought to have somebody waiting around for him who doesn't want him to die— don't you think?"

"Yeah, I do." Clark swallowed hard.

"Let's get moving, you guys," Piano Legs said, heading for the door.

They entered the waiting room cautiously, and for a while nobody said anything. Clark and Piano Legs stood against the wall as Steamboat continued his pacing.

"I'm sorry, Steamboat," Harry said quietly.

"You didn't show much sense, Harry."

"No, sir."

"You've got to try to protect them from themselves

sometimes. They may seem like tough little guys, Harry, but they really aren't. They're just kids." He stole a glance at Piano Legs, who was watching and listening intently. "They're trying to learn about life, about themselves. They get hurt, sometimes just inside, where it doesn't show. And they react, sometimes in ways that show very much. It's up to us to help them react to hurts in the right way. Every single kid—and counselor—has his own special hurts. We have to pay attention to what they're really saying to us, in so many ways."

Abruptly he stopped talking and looked away, afraid he was running off at the mouth from sheer anxiety about the hurt boy.

Clark took a tentative step toward Steamboat. "I didn't mean to hurt Bad Henry," he said earnestly. "It was just a fight, you know?"

"I know," Steamboat said. "But fighting didn't settle anything, did it? And it sure as heck left one boy hurt, whether you meant it or not. Was it worth it?"

"No!" Clark started to cry, wiping his tears away as fast as they appeared.

"Okay." Steamboat embraced him. "It's okay, Clark. All you can do now is try to learn from it, while we all hope for the best."

Steamboat studied the floor for a moment. Then he walked slowly over to his son. "Glad you came, Chet," he said quietly. "And glad you weren't responsible for this."

"What would you have done if I was?" There was a bitter edge to his voice.

"Told you the same thing I told Harry, except . . ."

"Except what?"

"Except that I would have also told you that I was sorry too, for what I may have done through the years to cause you to feel the way you do about people—about me. I would have told you . . ." Steamboat cleared his throat and went ahead hesitantly, trying not to think about what he was saying, so that he would say it naturally. ". . . that, well, I love you no matter what. Because you're my son."

Piano Legs whirled and dashed out through the door as if pursued by demons.

A few minutes later the doctor returned—this time smiling. "Well, folks, he just snapped out of it. There's no major damage indicated at all, just a minor concussion and a lump on the side of his head big as an egg. He'll have a headache for a while."

"Thank God he's okay!" Annie said breathlessly, putting a hand to her chest.

Bad Henrietta beamed with relief through her tears and hugged Annie.

"Can we see him?" Steamboat asked, feeling for the first time the cool sweat on his forehead.

"For a minute."

They followed the doctor down the corridor and into the room.

Bad Henry was propped up in bed, a big white bandage on his head. He opened his eyes slowly. Then he thrust out his lips pugnaciously. "Sis, what you doin' here? You got no business here."

"You chump!" she said brightly. "You do that again and it's gonna be *me* that comes upside your head!"

Annie and Steamboat laughed.

Steamboat put a hand on Henry's shoulder. "How are you, my boy?"

He shrugged. "Okay. Didn't hurt me none, nothin' I can't handle."

"We're all terribly sorry," Annie said, leaning over him. "You scared us for a while there."

"No reason to be scared. Can't nothin' hurt me bad."

Clark glanced at Steamboat and Annie, then down at Bad Henry. "I didn't mean to do it. I didn't mean to fight."

"Don't worry 'bout it. That's just one event. Come

Field Day, I'm gonna whip you at skateboarding and everything else."

"That's what *you* think, chump." Clark smiled and wiped away a tear.

"That's right. You're gonna be scared of me now."

"Scared of you?"

"That's right. 'Cause now you know I'm *hungry*." He started to laugh, then winced and touched his head.

The doctor moved in. "You'll all have to go home now so Henry can—"

"*Bad* Henry," said Bad Henry.

"Okay. So Bad Henry can get some rest."

"We'll see you in a couple of days," Steamboat said.

"You'll see me *tomorrow*! I ain't missin' Field Day for *nothin'*! I'm gonna dance on folks' heads! Ouch!" He touched his head again.

Out in the corridor, Clark walked with Steamboat. "How come him and me can't be friends?"

"Who says you're not?"

"Well, we had a fight, and—"

"Friends don't always have to be friendly—not every minute. They just have to be friends. Think about it."

Clark was thinking about it when the doors at the end of the corridor burst open and B.J. and Kiki came dashing through.

"Marian Pincu is gone!" B.J. cried, stopping them in their tracks.

"Gone?" Steamboat stared at the two counselors. "You mean ran away?"

"There wasn't any reason for her to run away," Kiki moaned. "Crazy Wilson must've got her!"

CHAPTER
8

Through most of the night, the entire camp scoured the adjacent woods, finding no leads to the whereabouts of Marian Pincu. There were no leads or clues other than the rumor about Crazy Wilson. To save strength and avoid anybody else's becoming lost, Steamboat called off the search a few hours before dawn, to resume it at daybreak.

Through this initial search, Charlie and Robin were nearly beside themselves with their private fears and worries and knowledge about Crazy Wilson. They were sworn to secrecy about him, of course. They prowled the woods along with the others, hoping, naturally, that Marian Pincu would be found, but also hoping that no one would pick up the trail to Crazy Wilson.

After everyone else had gone to bed, Charlie and Robin snuck out of camp.

They did not dare speak or turn on their flashlights until they had bumped and stumbled their way for several hundred yards. Then they panned their lights around.

"Are we lost?" Robin asked, peering along the beam of her light.

"No. It's this way. Come on."

They quickened their pace, ignoring the scratches and pricks and scrapes from brambles and branches, until they were on the seldom-used path that led to Crazy Wilson's cave.

They approached the entrance cautiously.

"Crazy Wilson?" Charlie called softly.

There was no answer from within, no sound at all except the gentle rustling of the fir branches overhead.

"Chief?"

"Wrrf."

His dog, Custer, trotted out of the mouth of the cave, wagging his tail. A moment later Crazy Wilson came slowly toward them, rubbing the sleep from his eyes.

"Well, well, well," the old Indian said, blinking, "looka who we got here. What brings you two out this time of night? More than just a friendly visit, I figger."

They stepped inside the cave, looked quickly around behind them to make sure nobody had followed, and switched off their lights.

Charlie briefly related the events of the evening, about the dance and the fight and the injury, and then the disappearance of Marian Pincu. Then he stopped.

The Indian carefully took the flashlight from Charlie's hand and switched it on, focusing the beam for a moment on Charlie's face. "It don't look like you've quite told all of it yet."

"Um, well, not exactly, Chief. That is, um, some people, er, a few in the camp, well, they suspect, that is—"

"Some people figger that maybe old Crazy Wilson had something to do with this here girl's mysterious disappearance, that it?"

"Well, yes, sir, that's right."

"We know it's not true!" Robin added quickly.

"Well, you're right, of course. No mystery there. But as a matter of fact I'm not too surprised at the suspicions. Legends are fun for a while, until something serious happens. Then legends turn dangerous. You two got any ideas about the girl?"

"No, sir," Charlie said, shaking his head sadly. "None at all. I hardly knew her."

"She's a nice girl," Robin said, "just a little spoiled is all. Nobody seems to have any ideas at all on what happened to her. She's just plain gone."

"I see." The Indian rubbed his chin thoughtfully. "Well, the truth is I know these woods like the back of my hand." He held out his broad, gnarled, dark hand and traced a finger along the back. "Every tree and brook and bush and nook and cranny. I suppose if she's out here somewhere I could find her. That what you got in mind?"

"Um, well, not exactly," Charlie said. "I mean, that isn't why we came. We came mostly to tell you about it. To warn you."

"We don't *want* you to search for her," Robin said. "We're afraid if you leave this cave they'll capture you!"

"Hmmph. Nobody gonna capture this old chief. Don't worry about *that*. But that don't seem to me to be important right now. More important than me is that little girl."

"We've already been out searching for her," Charlie said, "all of us. They called it off until daylight."

"Maybe she don't *want* to be found."

The two children blinked.

"But she was scared of the woods and the dark. Why wouldn't she want to be found?"

"Well, Robin, I figger you two probably know as much about that as anybody, bein' kids yourselves. I ain't been around kids—that is, not really *around* them—for a long time. Not since my own was . . ." His voice trailed off and he looked at the ground.

Charlie reached up and patted his arm. "It's not your fault. None of it."

For a moment they were silent.

Charlie turned away. "Everything's going wrong this year," he said softly.

"What do you mean?"

"Well, sir, the camp, everything. First the camp was in lousy shape when we got there. And there weren't enough campers—a lot of kids didn't come back this year. And now we heard . . ."

"Heard what?"

Charlie hesitated, hoping he wasn't saying something he shouldn't. "Steamboat himself said it. We heard him. The camp is finished. Dead. There's no more money."

"Old man Bolin's son won't keep it up?"

"Not only that," Robin said sorrowfully, "but he says he's going to sell the land so they can build, um, combonians on it."

"Combonians? You mean condominiums? Apartments?"

"Yes. He wants to sell it and make some profit. So that's the end of Camp Smilin' Through."

"And now this with Marian," Charlie said. "Everything's going wrong. Marian's gone, the camp will be gone, and they'll probably put you in jail."

Crazy Wilson frowned. "Not likely. None of it. But still, I see your point. Hmmm." He rubbed his chin and looked at the forlorn pair. "Come back with me, into the cave."

They trailed at his heels back to his room. The fire had burned low. He added a couple of logs and stood staring at the recovering flames. For a while he just stared. They looked at the fire and at him. His manner and bearing, for a time, commanded silence. He was, for all his age and lonesomeness, a powerful figure, his wrinkled brown skin and deeply furrowed brow lending him a true chiefly air.

Then he straightened, took a deep breath, and turned away from the fire. He went over to the wall to his pile of Indian things and removed the oilskin that covered them. He reached under his elegant headdress and pulled out a battered silver treasure tin the size of a shoe box.

He came back to the fire next to them and opened the box under their eyes.

The children peered into it. It contained a bear

claw, some arrowheads, a couple of gold nuggets, and —which caused them to wince—the dried head of an eagle.

He probed his fingers under those things and carefully extracted a rolled piece of parchment paper, brown around the edges and tied with a leather thong. He undid the thong and slowly unrolled the paper, smoothing the folds carefully so they didn't crack. He held it up in front of them.

"Read it, out loud."

Charlie squinted and read it slowly. "The governor of the United States Territory of California does hereby grant to the Chumash Chief Cat-Who-Runs-at-Night and his descendants, in perp . . . perp . . ."

"Perpetuity. Means forever."

". . . in perpetuity the land described hereafter."

"That's enough." He met their quizzical gaze. "The Chumash Chief Cat-Who-Runs-at-Night was my great-grandfather."

Their mouths fell open and they looked wide-eyed at each other.

"Yours?" Charlie choked.

"This is *your* land now?" Robin asked.

Crazy Wilson shrugged. "Who knows? All I know is what it says here. The paper's very old, as you can see. California wasn't even a state then. When a thing happened so long ago, sworn to by people no longer alive, it's tough to figger just what it might mean to-day. But I guess, if you trust this here piece of paper, it might still mean something."

"But why haven't you ever said anything about it to anybody?"

He shrugged again. "What's to say? Ownership never meant that much to me, long as things were going all right."

"But, but," Charlie stammered, "if it turned out that the land did belong to you, what would you do with it?"

Again he shrugged. "Do? Not much. Land is meant

to be land, way I figger it. I need a place to live my
way, and so do the bears and coyotes and the cats who
run at night. And white-eyed children like you need
a place where you can hear the wind and see the stars
and feel the earth."

"It's important to you then," Robin asked excitedly,
"about us, about the camp?"

He peered at them with narrowed eyes, sternly,
causing them to shrink back. "I reckon."

Charlie and Robin looked at the paper and each
other.

"But then—"

"We've got to—"

"Find out if this is any good!"

"I reckon. Here," he handed them the retied parchment, "take this with you. Find out what you can
find out."

They quickly started out of the cave, then stopped
and turned back.

"What about you?" Charlie asked.

"Me? Don't worry none. I may poke around the
woods a bit, or I might not. Depends on how I feel,
how the spirits move me, so to speak. I'll think on it
a while. You two be off, now, time's a-wasting. Go
on." He fluttered a hand at them and they raced out
of the cave.

It was, to be sure, a restless night, the rest of those
few hours before dawn, throughout the camp. But
perhaps the most restless of all was Piano Legs Scarborough. It was not just the sad accident at the dance
that caused him unrest. Or even that Marian Pincu
had disappeared. Or even that the camp was in trouble.

What lay beneath his inner turbulence was the
weight of things that had fallen on his father. Never
before had he sensed his father under such a combination of burdens, all at once. None of them, it
seemed, had been his father's fault. What's more, it

was a rare combination of pressures for which he himself, Chet Scarborough, was also blameless.

Or was he? Had his attitude and behavior somehow contributed to the distractions in the camp that had led to all these troubles? Had he somehow contributed to the unease that led to the fight, to a boy being in the hospital, to the camp becoming less attractive to other kids?

Was he, in fact, yet another drain upon his father's energies? In a way he wanted to think he was. To think that his father cared enough about him to expend some of his strength on concern for his son. In another way he didn't want to think so. He didn't want to be responsible for any of this. Not any of it.

Or else he wanted to share the burden.

Piano Legs thrashed in and out of dreams, in and out of sleep, in and out of his bunk. He quietly paced the floor, then lay back down.

Steamboat. Could anybody know how much it bothered him to have his father known as that? By everybody? By almost everybody except his son? A son couldn't call his father "Steamboat."

Not a bad nickname, but a nickname nonetheless. Nobody called him Mr. Scarborough except people who didn't know him or didn't care. Sometimes it would have been nice to hear someone say "Mr. Scarborough," or even, better yet, "Jack."

Steamboat and Piano Legs—like names of two nonpeople. It wasn't his fault that he was built the way he was, that he wasn't muscular through the chest and arms as was his father, or that he wasn't fast or a good tackler. "Steamboat" at least had a pleasant, friendly sound to it. "Piano Legs" served only to draw immediate attention to his strange and unwelcome build.

It was as if the two nicknames themselves served as a small wedge between him and his father.

But he knew that it wasn't the names that caused it. It was the way they were. Sometimes he didn't like his father—not because he wasn't a nice man, a good man, but because he was his *father*. And he had no allies in that attitude because, not only was Steamboat nobody else's father, but also everybody else liked him. Adored him.

Piano Legs, the son of the camp director, felt as lonely as an orphan.

It had been a good trick, dumping dirt in Hulk's bed. Sort of. But pointless. Nobody else even knew. So there had been no joy in seeing Hulk stomp around the cabin moaning and cursing while he dumped the junk off his cot. And besides, he had nothing against Hulk. Not really. Hulk was a better guy, was all. Deserved to be head counselor, just like his father said.

Piano Legs wanted more than anything else to be a better guy. More like Hulk. More like his father. But how? What kind of a move could he make toward that impossible goal?

He recalled his father's often-spoken instructions on the football practice field: "Snap the ball clean, square up, and hit the first guy closest to you. The rest of the play will take care of itself if everybody does his own job."

Which meant, in Piano Legs's present half-asleep perceptions, that you took on your own man, straight ahead, and beat him.

And his own man was himself.

When Charlie and Robin got back to camp at dawn, they were surprised to see half a dozen sheriff's cars in the parking lot and several uniformed men bustling around.

Annie came running over to them. "Where have you two been?"

"We have something important to tell you!" Charlie panted.

"About Crazy Wilson!" Robin said, also panting.

"What's going on? Marian Pincu is missing and everybody thinks Crazy Wilson kidnapped her."

"But he didn't!" Charlie cried.

"What? How do you know?"

"Because we know him," Robin said, beginning to calm down.

"We were just with him, and he wouldn't do that anyway," Charlie said.

"Because he's our friend," Robin added briskly.

"Friend?"

They nodded.

"Are they going to do something to him, Annie?"

"I don't know." She studied their faces. "What do you mean, he's your friend?"

"He *is*," they said together.

"I think you two better come inside with me. You're going to tell me everything you know about this." She aimed them ahead of her toward the cottage.

The sheriff's deputies and Steamboat and all the counselors set to combing the woods, small groups assigned to different quadrants according to an overall plan. Campers were ordered to stay behind in camp and just to keep an eye out.

The groups fanned out into the still-dark woods, crunching through the underbrush with deliberateness, poking under bushes with sticks, peering into crannies between rocks.

Deep in the woods, on his hillside, Crazy Wilson sat at the mouth of his cave, his hands clasped around his knees. Beside him, ears pricking up from time to time, lay Custer.

"Unh-hunh," the Indian said softly, reaching over to calm his restive dog, "I hear them. I think we better lay low a while, Custer."

He got up and moved around to gather some heavy foliage. He stacked it over the cave mouth, backing into the cave as he did so.

Just as the sun came up over the hills, Annie wheeled the pickup out the dirt road and onto the highway leading toward Los Angeles. Beside her, wearing expressions of weary hope, sat Robin and Charlie.

Their departure was not noticed by Steamboat, who at the time was with the assembled crews who had withdrawn from the initial search and were now awaiting carloads of fresh deputies in the parking lot.

Campers pressed around the action, eager to be as close to the officers and other searchers as possible.

"We'll find her," the grim-faced sheriff said. "I guarantee you. We'll start another search in the other quadrants as soon as we get the twelve fresh deputies here to relieve the first batch. And I'm hoping for some troops from the National Guard sometime this afternoon."

Steamboat, deep lines of weariness etched in his face, just nodded. "Field Day," he mumbled.

Now another car pulled into the parking lot, trailing a plume of dust. It skidded to a stop and a well-dressed but haggard couple jumped out and came running over to Steamboat.

"Mr. and Mrs. Pincu," Steamboat said to the sheriff. "Have you found Marian?" cried the woman, grabbing Steamboat's arm. "Have you?"

"Not yet, Mrs. Pincu," he said as gently as he could. "Not yet. We will. Glad you're here. Sorry about everything."

She broke into tears and sank her head against the shoulder of her husband, who himself was teary-eyed but trying to retain composure.

"What have you done so far, Steamboat?" Mr. Pincu asked.

"Searched. We were out almost all night, again at dawn. Some deputies are still out there. When we get a new crew, we'll all head out again. No sign of anything."

"No indication at all of foul play, so far," the sheriff said, meaning to be consoling but instead causing a new outbreak of sobbing from Mrs. Pincu.

"Hulk!"

"Yes, Steamboat?" Hulk trotted over.

"Get all the kids to the council ring. Wait with them there. Soon as the new deputies get here and we get 'em dispatched on search patterns, I'll be over."

"Right." He turned to the throng. "Okay, everybody, follow me! Everybody to the council ring! Pronto!"

All the campers scampered off behind Hulk.

The wait for the new deputies seemed long. Twice the sheriff went to his radio to see what was delaying them. At last they arrived and quickly assembled around the sheriff and Steamboat for instructions.

Shortly Annie pulled up in the pickup with Robin and Charlie. They parked away from the other cars, and Annie hustled them out of the parking lot and off to the cottage to enter the back door.

A few brief moments later, Charlie and Robin emerged from that door and dashed off into the woods.

When they arrived at Crazy Wilson's cave, they stopped, momentarily puzzled by the foliage camouflaging the opening. They called to him. Getting no answer, they pushed aside the growth and went in.

They found him sitting by his campfire, casually eating some cooked vegetables from a bowl.

"You're okay!" Charlie said.

" 'Course. Why not?"

"You didn't answer."

"Can't hear much with that stuff over the entrance. What's up? They find the girl?"

"No. But—"

"The paper's good!" Robin sang, causing Custer to leap up and lick her hand.

Charlie handed him the parchment.

Crazy Wilson stared at the paper as if seeing it for the first time. "Good? It's good?"

"We went to a man who's a friend of Robin's father who's in the state legislature and he says it's good!" Charlie said.

"Hold on, slow up." Crazy Wilson shook his head as if to clear it. "What's that now?"

"It'll stand up in court, the man said!" Robin waved her arms excitedly. "It's legal!"

"Well, now, my, my, my." The old Indian just sat there shaking his head and staring at the paper. "Imagine that."

"The land is yours!"

"Well, I'll be."

"It all belongs to you!"

"After all this time. My, my."

"In perp . . ."

"Perpetuity, Charlie, my friend. Perpetuity. Imagine that." He sighed and shook his head.

"But there's still a problem," Charlie added hastily, lowering his voice.

Crazy Wilson looked up at him.

"The police are looking for you," Robin said.

"They still think you kidnapped the girl—maybe."

"I see. That's no good." He stared at the fire and slowly put the precious paper down beside him. "I've got to go help find the girl."

"No," Charlie pleaded, "don't go!"

"They'll arrest you!" Robin crouched down beside him.

"Well, I have to do what I have to do." The Indian got languorously to his feet, stretching his lean frame. "I have to go. Now, you children go on back to camp. I'll handle this. I'll do it my way."

"But—"

"Go. I ain't a chief for nothing. I can handle my end."

Reluctantly, the two left and headed back toward camp, taking care to elude the search parties.

Now Crazy Wilson put the paper back into his treasure tin and closed it carefully. He held it up to the light of the fire and turned it slowly in his hands, studying it from every side. Then he went over to his pile of Indian wear and put the box back under his headdress.

He knelt there beside the pile of old precious things, stroking the eagle feathers with one hand and Custer with the other, with a silent reverence.

Back at camp, all the kids were gathered at the council ring. They fidgeted and shuffled their feet nervously, though abiding by Hulk's prohibition against walking around.

For them, the wait for Steamboat's appearance was interminable. Orphans muttered to orphans, old campers muttered among themselves. This was supposed to be Field Day. But, like everything else this camp session, it certainly wasn't going according to plan.

Steamboat plodded into the cottage, Mr. and Mrs. Pincu and the sheriff behind him. "Annie? Annie?"

She came out of the back room.

"Where you been, Annie?"

"Doing something important. Have Robin and Charlie got back yet?"

"Back? Where'd they go?"

"The woods."

"But what the devil were they doing. They're not supposed to be—"

"They were doing something important too. They should be back any minute. Let's get over to the council ring."

Steamboat gritted his teeth, confused and impatient, but too tired to question further.

He strode into the center of the ring, and the crowd immediately hushed.

"Now, you all know that Marian Pincu is missing. You know we've spent the night looking for her, and others are looking for her right now. You kids leave that to us. None of you is to leave this immediate area. Everybody got that?"

The kids, now looking a bit frightened, nodded.

"Now then. This is Mr. and Mrs. Pincu. This is a

very difficult time for them. I don't want anybody bothering them, not to ask questions, not to say anything. Got that?"

They all nodded, some daring to peek at the sad, reddened, puffy, teary faces of Mr. and Mrs. Pincu, who stood behind Steamboat holding hands.

"Now." Steamboat directed a fierce gaze around the ring. "I've asked you before, and I'm going to ask you again now. Is there anybody here who knows anything about this that you haven't told me? Anybody?"

All faces looked down.

"This is the most important question I've ever asked any of you. And it's more important than any of *you*, right now. Anybody got anything to say?"

Nobody said anything.

"All right. I believe you. So the situation is, all of you will stay here. I and the counselors will join the deputies to continue the search. Except for Chet." His eyes landed on his son. "Chet will stay here with you."

"But—" Piano Legs looked up pleadingly.

"Everybody got that?"

The kids nodded.

"Chet?"

Piano Legs nodded.

"Okay, then, I'll see you all a little—"

"We saw him! We saw him!"

Charlie and Robin came running into the ring.

"What the—"

"We were just with him!" Charlie cried.

"Crazy Wilson didn't do it!" Robin yelped.

Steamboat grabbed his head. "What are you talking about? What's going on?"

"We just saw him!" Robin went on. "We were with him! He's our friend!"

"He lives in a cave," Charlie continued, "and he has a nice old dog that's the Hound of Death only he's really just a nice old dog named Custer and—"

"What in—"

"And he owns the land!" Robin bellowed.

"This land!" Charlie echoed her.

"Now just a minute!" Steamboat grabbed Charlie's shoulders.

"The kids are right," Annie put in. "Every word is true."

"But, but—" Steamboat let Charlie go and put both hands to his head, staggering a bit. "What in blazes is everybody trying to say around here?"

Now Kiki Watwood came up to him, holding the hands of Della Chesbro and LaVerne Seeds, both girls crying.

"Steamboat?" Kiki said softly.

"Not now, not now!" Steamboat elbowed her away. "What do you mean, Crazy Wilson owns this land? Freddy Bolin owns it."

"No, he doesn't!" Charlie said.

Kiki pressed forward again, this time tugging on Steamboat's sleeve. "Steamboat, it's about Marian!"

"Hunh?" He turned toward her, blinking. "What?"

"Crazy Wilson didn't kidnap her. She ran away."

"Hunh?"

"Della and LaVerne just told me, and it's all my fault. They were afraid to say anything before. We all made them afraid. Including me."

Steamboat breathed heavily for a few moments, looking at the two tearful orphan girls. "Okay," he said softly, "tell me now."

Mr. and Mrs. Pincu pushed in. "What is it?" she asked urgently. "Something about Marian?"

"Did you find her?" Mr. Pincu pleaded.

"No, sir," Kiki said, sadly shaking her head. "But I know she ran away. Della and LaVerne saw her go. They told her that her parents were dead."

Mrs. Pincu stepped back as if struck, a hand to her mouth. "But why? Why would you do a thing like that?"

The girls broke into heavy sobbing.

"We didn't mean nothing," Della sputtered. "We ain't got no parents and she was always talkin' about hers."

"So we just told her that to get even," LaVerne blubbered. "We didn't mean for nothing to happen to her!"

"We didn't want no Crazy Wilson to get her, and—"

"Okay, that's enough," Steamboat said, putting his hands on their shoulders.

Now Kiki burst into tears. "It's all my fault! I didn't do anything to keep it from happening!" I should have paid attention. I should have done something. I should have cared more about what was going on. It's my fault!" She slapped her fists against her thighs.

Annie put an arm around Kiki.

"Well, I'll be double-blasted." Steamboat looked from one face to the other, at Charlie and Robin, at Annie. "You mean she's just run off someplace?"

"Is that what you mean?" Mrs. Pincu put in urgently. "She's just lost?" She gave her husband a hopeful look.

The sheriff, who had been quietly communicating with his men in the woods, now took the walkie-talkie away from his ear. "Well, we still got to keep looking, Steamboat. And I wouldn't write off the possibility that the old Indian did get hold of her— not that he would do anything bad, necessarily."

"He didn't!" Charlie yelled. "He didn't get hold of her! He didn't do anything!"

"Well—"

"I doubt Crazy Wilson had anything to do with this," Steamboat said, "from all I've just heard and all I know."

"He didn't!"

"Okay. All right." Steamboat turned to face the campers. "Everybody, listen up. I'm changing our plans a little. We're going to organize everybody into a gigantic search party. We've got good light now, and with so many of us in the woods, nobody should lose sight of the rest. We'll try it for a while, see what we come up with. Everybody fall in behind your counselors!"

The group scrambled into place, excited with the prospects of the search, albeit a little confused from the revelations of Charlie and Robin, and Della and LaVerne.

"Move out!"

Trailing their counselors single file, the groups marched off through the camp toward the woods.

Except for Dee Dee and Dianne. Lingering at the rear, they were glad to see nobody look back.

"Not me," Dee Dee whispered. "I'm not gonna thrash around out in the woods and ruin my clothes and get all sweaty just for some miserable snot-nose."

"Me neither."

They dropped farther and farther back, and then, unnoticed, slipped off in the direction of the waterfront.

Giggling over the ease of their escape, and the wisdom of it, they trotted past the dock down the beach to where they couldn't be seen by anybody checking back at the council ring.

"This was one of my better ideas," Dee Dee said. "I need a smoke."

"Me too."

"Hogwash. You don't smoke."

"I want to."

"Okay."

A few yards ahead of them lay the old war canoe where it had been dragged ashore after the hilarious sinking and turned upside down to await repairs.

"There," Dee Dee said, pointing to it. "Let's hide in there and have ourselves some smokes."

"Okay. Where are your cigarettes? You don't have any pockets."

" 'Course not, silly. *Here*." She reached down the

front of her blouse and extracted a pack. "Great hiding place, plus it helps the way you look, if you know what I mean."

They giggled.

"You crawl under, then hold it up for me."

"Okay."

As Dee Dee lifted the bow, Dianne dropped to her knees and started under. Suddenly she stopped. "Dee Dee! Look!"

Huddled under the canoe, shivering from the long night and the fright and the loneliness, was Marian, holding her breath.

It took but a few moments of running and yowling and screeching to summon all the searchers back from the woods. Everybody massed around the girls, hollering, moaning, praising, thanking. Mr. and Mrs. Pincu hugged Marian, who was hiccuping and crying too much to talk.

Della and LaVerne, too, threw their arms around the shaking girl.

Dee Dee and Dianne, the unwitting heroes of the moment, basked in the praise.

"It was nothing really," Dee Dee said, lowering her head modestly. "Just an idea I had, that she might be down there."

"Only place we didn't think of," Steamboat said, beaming.

Mr. and Mrs. Pincu blubbered and cooed over their daughter. "You want a brownie?" Mrs. Pincu asked.

"No," Marian said firmly, her first words since disappearing.

As everybody calmed down, Steamboat looked around. "Well, that's that part of it. Where are Charlie and Robin?"

"Here, sir," they said, stepping forward hand in hand.

"Good. Now I think we need to have some other things cleared up. What was all that about—"

"Look, Charlie, look!" Robin pointed toward the edge of the woods.

Just emerging from the dense growth came a majestic Indian chief. The entire camp fell absolutely silent, leaving the only sounds those of his moccasins crunching on the twigs.

CHAPTER
9

He was clad head to toe in buckskin, his finest chief's finery. His silver jewelry tinkled against his beads. On his magnificent headdress the eagle feathers danced and glinted in the sun.

"Our friend, Crazy Wilson!" Charlie and Robin sang proudly. They ran up to him, took his hands, and led him over to Steamboat, while throughout the camp, mouths formed silently the awesome words, "Crazy Wilson."

Steamboat was stunned at the appearance of the old Indian he had seen previously only once or twice, and never in this kingly outfit, and certainly never in the camp. "Crazy Wilson," he said softly.

"That's me. See you found the girl. That's good." He looked around at the assembly, nodding without smiling, maintaining a stern and glorious image of strength and dignity. "Saves me the trouble. Yes." He fixed his clear eyes on Steamboat. "I'm Crazy Wilson. My white man's name is Herbert Wilson. It's your doing I'm called Crazy."

"No, no, I didn't—"

"Don't matter." He held up his hand, causing his jewelry to jingle. "I ain't offended. Herbert ain't such a great name either. My tribal name is Washakie. It means Elk-Standing-in-Sunshine. I am the hereditary chief of the Chumash Tribe of the Iroquois Nation."

Several quiet oohs and aahs filtered from the crowd.

"Chief?" Steamboat's eyes widened.

"My friends in the camp, Charlie and Robin"—

several heads turned toward the quickly notorious pair—"tell me they have spoken to a white lawmaker, and that an old land grant I hold is good. Your camp is on my land."

"Hunh?" Steamboat was bewildered. "What lawmaker? What land grant?"

"Annie took us," Charlie said.

Annie nodded in affirmation.

"A friend of my father's," Robin explained. "He lives not far from here. He's a state senator and a lawyer and he knows all about Indian stuff."

"When? When did you go?"

"Last night," Annie said, "or actually early this morning. But we'll tell you all those details later. It's true, you can trust it."

"See," Robin said excitedly, "Crazy Wilson—oh, I'm sorry, I mean Chief Elk-Standing-in-Sunshine—has a paper that says his great-grandfather and all his descendants own this land. And the paper is real!"

"He owns the land!" Charlie chirped.

"Hold it." Steamboat slowly sat down on a log. "Wait a minute. What about Freddy Bolin?"

"He never owned it," Charlie said. "Nobody ever really did except the chiefs."

Steamboat eyed the Indian uncertainly. "But how come Freddy, or Freddy's father, thought they owned the land? How did all this happen?"

Crazy Wilson shrugged. "You know how things go, Steamboat. Somebody comes along, some kind of pioneer type or something, sees some woods out here in the wilds of a place not yet the state of California, and just takes it, files a deed, and there you have it. Nobody questioned it all these years, I guess. No reason to. Who owned it never even mattered to me—until now. Now it matters."

Steamboat rubbed his head. "What are you going to do with it? You going to sell it?"

"Oh, no, no, no. Just keep it the way it is." He squared his shoulders and looked off into the distance.

"A lot of dishonorable things have happened to tribal land, as I guess you know. Nothing much can be done about that. Been a lot of progress, lot more people, cars, and all the rest. Now, a lot of city-type folks concern themselves with all the problems of the world. But not me. I'm too simple. My world is just this area here." He swept his arms around grandly, taking in the entire camp and woods. "Just where I live. And I don't want much for myself. This here is plenty. And it is mine. My tribal land will not have apartments and shopping centers on it. It is for me to live on. And it is for your camp, if you still want to have it here."

The words sunk into Steamboat slowly. Then he began to smile. "Oh yes," he said at last. "Yes, yes, yes!" He jumped up, waving his fists in the air. "We want our camp! Everybody!" He whirled around, waving the campers to their feet. "Do we want our camp? Come on, show how much we want our camp!"

Cheers resounded around the council ring.

Crazy Wilson raised his arms, silencing them. He looked around somberly at the happy faces. "I hereby proclaim that Charlie and Robin are honorary Chumash Indians." Then he added, under his breath to Steamboat, "One chief and no Indians is a lousy ratio. Couple of honoraries ain't much better, but it's better than nothing—and more than I had before." Then he broke into a warm smile and reached out to clasp Steamboat's hand.

"Do I have to be a squaw?" Robin asked, wrinkling up her nose.

Crazy Wilson laughed. "Well, times change. No, you can both be braves if you want."

Charlie and Robin hugged each other and danced around like Indians.

"One last thing," the Indian said, holding up a hand. "Something about this camp has always bothered me."

Faces fell.

"What bothered me was your dad-blamed *name*. I want you to give the camp a more dignified name."

"What kind of name?" Steamboat asked warily.

"You may use my name if you like," Crazy Wilson said, coolly studying his fingernails.

"Camp Elk-Standing-in-Sunshine?"

"Well, that does sound a bit cumbersome, I'll admit. So why not call it my Indian name? Why not Camp Washakie?"

Steamboat reflected for a moment. "Camp Washakie." Then he grinned and stuck out a hand again to Crazy Wilson. "Camp Washakie it is! Fantastic!"

The campers cheered themselves almost hoarse, until Crazy Wilson again spread his arms. In solemn tones, looking skyward, he said something in his native tongue.

"What does that mean, Chief?"

"Yesterday wood, tomorrow ashes; the fire is only today."

Then, as all faces were fixed on him in awe, the old man turned and strode deliberately off toward the woods. In silence, they all watched him go, heard the tinkling of his beads and the crunch of his moccasins. No one else made a sound until he had completely disappeared back into his tree-shrouded land.

Steamboat took a deep breath. He looked at the sky, then at the campers. "Well, kids, it looks like we still have a camp, and today is still Field Day. Everybody participates. The teams are posted on the bulletin boards, the rosters of the blue team and the green team. Baseball, tug-o-war, canoeing, and skateboarding this afternoon. Tonight, the biggie—capture-the-flag. We'll see everybody on the playing field in an hour."

Slowly, almost reluctantly, the council ring broke up. The campers had been nearly overwhelmed by everything that had happened. The return to Field Day came almost too suddenly. And with that, there came some recollections of how things were at the camp—not all things were good.

Hulk sidled up to Vance. "You think these jerks are gonna try to kill each other today?"

"Who? What do you mean?"

"I mean that we still got a camp full of two opposing sides—and I don't mean blue against green. Still a lot of grudges."

"Hey, we just gotta keep on top of them, that's all. It's our responsibility to keep things under control. Listen, we're going to make sure *all* these kids have a good Field Day."

"Okay. We'll try, at least."

Steamboat stepped into the Iroquois cabin to find Alan, Hayden, Preston, and little Joe Louis. "Hey, boys, how've things been with Piano Legs lately? He been treating you all right?"

The boys smiled at each other.

"He's been terrific, just fine," Joe said, "ever since he somehow just seemed to come to understand how it felt to be treated bad."

"Great," Steamboat said, "glad to hear it."

He met Piano Legs coming up the path. "Your boys tell me everything's going fine," he said, throwing an arm around him. "Glad to hear you're treating them better."

Piano Legs blushed at the memory of how the little boys had trussed him up and treated him to a swirly. "Yeah."

"See how things work out when you try?"

"Yeah." He pulled away slowly, wishing for a time when such compliments could be deserved. "I better get the guys ready for Field Day."

"Okay, see you later."

He watched his father disappear around the dining hall. Then he saw Dogbreath Mooney come along the path. Piano Legs grimaced at the thought of Dogbreath's unique weaponry. "Hey, Dogbreath," he called, "come here."

"Why?"

"Just come over here."

Dogbreath came cautiously over.

As soon as he was within reach, Piano Legs spun him around, grabbed him by the collar, and marched him off toward the lavatory.

"What you gonna do?" Dogbreath whined.

"You'll see."

"You're gonna give me a swirly!" Dogbreath shot acrid breaths out right and left.

But Piano Legs, holding his own breath, shoved him through the door and bent him down over the sink. Holding him by the back of the neck and ignoring the sputtering oaths the boy tried to shout, he smeared a bar of soap across Dogbreath's teeth and rubbed the suds in harshly. Then he splashed some water on to rinse, and let him straighten up.

Dogbreath was speechless—nearly breathless.

While the boy was panting to recover, Piano Legs took a brand-new toothbrush from his back pocket, and a tiny new tube of paste, and slapped them into Dogbreath's hand. "Here. Use it while you're hanging up."

"Hanging up?"

"Right." Piano Legs hoisted him by the seat of the pants and slipped his belt over a towel hook, leaving him dangling just off the floor. "Now, brush your teeth."

"Hunh?" Dogbreath looked at the toothbrush as if it were some kind of detestable foreign tool.

"Brush!"

Swinging his legs angrily, Dogbreath squeezed some toothpaste onto the brush and began savagely brushing his teeth, spewing out clouds of foam from his mouth.

"Good. Just keep brushing until somebody comes in here and gets you down."

"You can't get away with this!"

"Keep brushing," Piano Legs said as he sauntered

out of the lavatory. "This is making new men out of us both."

Piano Legs strode merrily up the path to his cabin, pleased to feel he was now on the right track toward helping the camp along.

Steamboat was about to enter his cottage when he stopped short. He saw Freddy Bolin and his friend Hal just getting out of their car.

"What's new, Steamboat?" Freddy said, smiling as they approached.

"Not much."

"We just dropped by so you can show us how we're going to pick up our fifteen percent profit, then we'll be on our way."

"Oh," Steamboat said, smirking, "it's fifteen percent now, is it?"

"That's right. That's what we said, wasn't it, Hal?"

Hal nodded with his usual tight-lipped grimness.

"Unh-hunh." Steamboat smiled. "You know, Freddy, I've got a funny story for you, really interesting."

"Well, we're really just interested in the profit picture right now—kind of rushed."

"I'm gonna tell you a funny story anyhow." Steamboat narrowed his eyes a bit. "You remember Crazy Wilson?"

"Yeah, why?"

"That old Indian has a piece of paper that says all this land was granted to his great-grandfather by the governor of California back when it was a territory."

"What?" Freddy looked puzzled.

"Yeah, and what's really interesting is that his piece of paper is as good as gold and will stand up in court. What that means, Freddy-boy, is that you don't own this land and neither did your father— God rest his good and honest and innocent soul."

Freddy stepped backward, a hand to the side of his face as if he had felt a blow.

"So, see, Freddy? Isn't that a funny story? True, however, and it's all been checked out at the state legislature. Isn't that funny? Why aren't you laughing, Freddy, like I am?" Steamboat emitted a low, growling laugh.

"No," Freddy mumbled. "It can't be."

"Can. Is." Steamboat reached out and tapped Freddy's shoulder, causing the thin man to jump. "You were a weak little boy and I'm afraid you grew up to be a weak man. I hope you don't ruin your life letting people like your friend here run it for you."

Hal tried one of his deepest scowls, but Steamboat squared off in front of him, puffed up his barrel chest, and tightened his mighty arms. Hal sighed.

"I don't believe any of this!" Freddy hissed.

Steamboat waved his hand. "Believe what you want. My new landlord says I can stay here, and I always go along with my landlord, right? Anyway, I rather imagine Crazy Wilson and I will be seeing you in court, sometime up the line. Meanwhile," he turned to Hal, "Hal, you ever been to summer camp?"

Hal shook his head slightly.

"Well, now, that's an experience you shouldn't be without. And this here is one of the best. I want you to enjoy our fine facilities here."

And with that, Steamboat grabbed the silent man by the scruff of his neck and propelled him forward down toward the dock.

Campers came running from all directions to watch the spectacle while Freddy danced spastically along behind, waving his arms and sputtering.

Steamboat marched Hal to the dock, out along it, and then heaved him ingloriously off the end.

No sooner had Hal hit the water than Piano Legs came running down the skateboard track. Barely slowing his pace, he grabbed Freddy, swung him onto the dock, and, using his huge strong right leg, booted him off the end.

"Chet!" Steamboat gasped as he watched the two men flailing in the water. "Why'd you do that?"

"Just thought I'd help you tidy up the camp," Piano Legs said, grinning.

"Well, I'll be!"

Father and son strode back off the dock to meet a crowd of delighted campers.

"Well, kids," Steamboat hollered, "it's Field Day! Let's get it rolling! Blue team against the green team. Everybody plays! Baseball first! Onto the field!"

"Wait a minute!" Luscious Moncrief barked. "Can I talk?"

"Sure," Steamboat said.

"Ain't gonna be no green and blue."

"What?"

"I mean, ain't gonna be no jive Iroquois against no turkey Navajos and all that garbage. We got too many unsettled scores here, too much gone down already. We got to find out who's really the best."

"Now, just a minute—"

"So it's gonna be them against us! The White-Eyes against the Watusis!"

Before Steamboat could respond, others chimed in.

"We want it that way too, Steamboat," Bobby said, pushing through the throng. "Us against them."

"C'mon, Steamboat," Bad Henrietta shouted, jumping up and down, "let us divide ourselves up however we want!"

Sateen, Michelle, Clark, Bad Henry, and Paper Lady picked up the hollering in favor of the idea, soon joined by almost all the campers.

Steamboat scratched his head and waved them quiet. "Listen, kids, I've been a football coach for a long time, and camp director too. To me, winning isn't as important as it is to other people. Sports and camp ought just to be fun."

The campers renewed their clamor. "Let us do it! We want to do it! It'll be fun!" Even the littlest kids were now joining in.

"Okay, okay, knock it off! I'm going to turn this thing over to the counselors. I don't want you doing it this way, but I'm not going to stop you either. Hulk, whatever you decide will be the way it's done."

"Yes, sir."

Steamboat stalked out of the ring, up the path toward his cottage, followed quickly by Annie.

"Do you think I copped out?" he asked her.

"Do *you* think you did?"

"I'm not sure. But Hulk's my man. In fact, I sensed a good attitude out there among the counselors—all of them. They'll do what's best. And when they need me, I'll be there."

"You know what, Steamboat?" She took his hand. "You're a very special camp director."

"With you here, I manage."

Back at the council ring, all the clamor was now directed at Hulk, who let it rage for a minute, then held up his hand for silence. "Okay, listen, you guys. This is Steamboat's camp. What he says oughta go, right?"

"We wanna do it!" Bobby persisted. "We all dig Steamboat, but this ain't got nothing to do with him."

"Hold it! Everything here has something to do with Steamboat, so you can get that idea out of your head. I've been working with him for a long time, and I've heard him say a hundred times that winning and trying to settle grudges that way is not good. I've heard him say a hundred times also that what the kids want to do in this camp is what they ought to do —so long as it isn't destructive. That is a strong man that can allow so much freedom. He takes a tremendous responsibility on himself—more than they dare in other camps. Steamboat is the spirit of this place— don't you ever forget it."

"Right!" Piano Legs found himself saying.

Hulk nodded around at the other counselors. Everybody was with him. So were the campers.

"Now. Steamboat put me in charge of this particu-

lar matter. All right. So here it is. As long as nobody
sits around their cabins, as long as we all have the
real spirit of Camp Smilin' Through in this particular Field Day, the teams for today's events will be—
White-Eyes and Watusis!"

Orphans and old campers alike leaped up and down
and cheered, then quickly separated into the two
teams and headed for the baseball diamond.

The baseball game was a wild, free-swinging affair
—in the broadest meaning of the words. There were
plenty of hitters—Luscious, Doctor Death, Jet-Man,
and Bad Henry for the Watusis, equaled at the plate
by Bobby, Clark, Wolfman, and Turkey. Bad Henrietta and Sateen were almost as good with the bat for
the Watusis, while Michelle was the only White-Eyed
girl who could really hold her own.

But not all the swinging was at the plate. Hulk, the
umpire, had his hands full not only calling balls and
strikes but also breaking up fights. In the third inning,
Luscious hit Bobby in the shoulder with a high inside
fast ball, and Bobby tossed down his bat and stormed
toward the mound, restrained at the last yard by
Hulk, who steered him back to the plate.

In the next inning, Bobby retaliated with a pitch
that just missed Luscious's head. The two managed to
run together and grapple and swing a few harmless
open hands at each other before Hulk and Vance
intervened.

The game went on in a loose style, with intermit-
tent trips, slaps, kicks, and lunges that, while not
evolving into outright fights, implied that the day's
competition would not be friendly.

The orphans won it when Luscious powdered one
over center field with the bases loaded.

The final score of 20-16 seemed to settle nothing,
and left Hulk shaking his sweaty head and wondering
if he'd made the right decision by letting the campers
divide up as they had.

Skateboarding was not so close. Jet-Man surprised everybody but himself and Doctor Death by winning the speed run. But in the slalom and free style—his specialties—Clark Brunkhorst won easily. His final handstand put the White-Eyes well into the lead, and his teammates mopped up the rest of the inexperienced Watusis.

Canoeing and the tug-o-war were next. Bobby, Clark, Wolfman, and Turkey—the best White-Eye athletes—huddled.

"We'll win the canoeing and they'll probably win the tug-o-war because our little kids ain't worth a diddle-darn," Bobby said.

"Yeah, they got all the strength," Turkey said. "They sure grow orphans strong around here."

"So it's gonna come down to capture-the-flag," Bobby said, adding, with a mean smile, "so tonight it's for blood."

They all shook hands.

In the canoeing, James Jefferson and Joe Louis won early heats, surprisingly, as did Bad Henrietta. Others, such as Robin, Wolfman, and Bobby, won as expected. Bobby reached the finals by beating Wolfman. But then Bad Henrietta upset Robin, the strong favorite, in the other semifinal.

The final pitted Bad Henrietta against Bobby Stenzel.

"She's got nothin' in this," Bobby whispered to Wolfman. "I'll murder her."

Bobby took a quick early lead. He let Bad Henrietta close to a half length, then, smiling back at her, he pulled easily away again.

But then, while Bad Henrietta diligently plowed ahead, never losing her concentration, Bobby began showing off, trying some fancy strokes. He pulled a couple of crabs with his paddle, splashing water badly, and Henrietta began to come on. Taking advantage of his mistakes, never looking up, straining at her paddle, and remembering the techniques she had watched Robin demonstrate for the last many days, she suddenly forged ahead by a nose.

Bobby was unnerved and lost his rhythm entirely. Bad Henrietta sailed past him and flew over the finish line going away.

When they returned to shore, the orphans mobbed Henrietta triumphantly, while the White-Eyes milled around Bobby silently, slumping as he did in despair.

To even things up before the capture-the-flag, the White-Eyes would have to win the tug-o-war, which seemed impossible against the orphans' muscle.

Bad Henrietta, exhausted but standing tall with pride, tapped Gerri Belardi on the shoulder. "Hey, honey, you been askin' people all along if they're interested in track. How come you never asked me?"

"You? Gee, I never thought you'd be interested."

"Why not? Ain't I built right or something?"

"Yes, sure, you sure are. Are you interested?"

"Yeah, I'm interested."

"Maybe you could work out with me, okay?"

"You got it, sister!"

For the tug-o-war the counselors had dug a long, straight trench and filled it with water. Now the kids lined up, the teams facing each other along an old inch-thick rope.

Bad Henry was the lead man for the Watusis, Clark for the White-Eyes. Bobby anchored at the far end of the rope for his team, Luscious for his. All the others, including the little ones, were positioned between their leads and anchors.

Hulk knotted a bandanna to the exact center of the rope. Vance took his judge's stance there.

"You little guys don't quit on me!" Bobby hollered as he took his grip on the rope and dug in his feet.

"We gonna bury 'em!" Luscious shouted as he prepared the same way at the opposite end.

Confidentially to Clark, Bobby muttered, "They're gonna kill us."

"We'll give it what we got, at least," Clark said.

Vance looked right and left. "All right? Go!"

Immediately the orphans surged back, pulling the bandanna a good two feet their way. In three seconds the old campers were on the verge of defeat.

And they would have been beaten, too, right then and there, except for Bobby's exhortations and refusal to give up. Spurred by the feeling that he had already been the goat in two events, Bobby yelled, "Hang on! Pull, you little jerks. Pull or I'll swirly you into next week!"

They pulled. The rope stopped sliding. The bandanna stopped just short of the victory line.

Some of the smaller White-Eyes began to cry from exertion. Now Clark Brunkhorst wouldn't let them quit. "Get on that rope! Pull!"

Luscious rallied the orphans. "We almost got 'em! They got no willpower! One more time! Pull!"

Some of the smaller ones on both sides dropped their holds and flopped into the mud, too tired to continue. The orphans gained another inch.

Then again the rope stopped. Doctor Death, just in front of Luscious, had let his hands slip on the line.

"Pull, man!" Luscious roared. "You lettin' us down!"

"Don't yell at me, man! I'm a mathematician, not an athlete!"

"Pull now, count later, Doctor Jive! Else I'll subtract your teeth from your mouth!"

"Now that you explained it . . ." Doctor Death heaved anew on the line.

The bandanna wavered near the victory mark for the Watusis. Suddenly Gale Pincu emitted a loud groan and rolled off to the side, his fat body pumping for air.

"Pincu!" Bobby screeched. "Get back in there! For once we need your flab!"

Gale shook his head.

Luscious couldn't stand the sight of such weakness.

"Pincu, you fat, dumb, weak honky, your mama musta been a toad!"

Gale sat up. "Hunh? What'd you say? Don't you ever say that!" He lunged back for the rope and gave it such an adrenaline-backed yank that both teams lost their balance.

"Don't you ever say anything about my mama!" he yowled, pulling even more savagely.

Now the bandanna began for the first time to move the White-Eyes' way. Then it moved faster. With one last gigantic heave combining the muscle of Clark, Wolfman, Bobby, and Gale, the rope slid several feet, and the orphans were tumbled forward into the trench.

Gale dropped the rope, leaped in among them, and began thumping Luscious on the head.

The counselors broke it up in seconds.

"We won!" Bobby screamed, dancing up and down in the trench. "We won! We won!"

And indeed they had. Bobby collapsed in a heap, as did everybody else on both sides. The score of Field Day was now 2-2. Left was only capture-the-flag, to take place that night.

The teams wolfed down hot dogs in separate ends of the dining halls. In the boys' hall, captains plotted strategy for the final competition. At neither end of the room was the tone decidedly friendly.

"We gotta teach them honkies a lesson," Luscious said. "See what they tried to do to Bad Henry down there? And him with a bad head?"

"My head's okay," Bad Henry said grumpily.

"Yeah, but we got some scores to settle."

"Precisely what we got to settle," Doctor Death said, "is the score of two-to-two."

"Don't take no mathematician to figure *that* out," Jet-Man said. "Even *White-Eyes* can add that up. What we need is speed. I'm gonna get that rag they call their flag!"

"Well, we're faster and stronger than they are," Luscious said.

"And badder," added Bad Henry.

"Maybe a couple busted heads would show them jive turkeys who's boss, out there in the dark."

He proceeded to sketch some military-type patrol actions on a napkin as the other orphans leaned over to watch.

At the other end of the hall, Bobby was sketching too. "What we got on them is brains," he said. "We'll outthink 'em."

"That shouldn't be too difficult," Gale Pincu pronounced, still glowing from his contribution at tug-o-war.

"I'd like to get ahold of that Bad Henrietta," Michelle growled, "and plant her like a tree." Michelle, disdaining the relatively nonathletic girls, had drifted over to the boys' hall determined to stir the White-Eyes to meaner heights.

"We gotta watch out for rough stuff," Clark said soberly. "You know how they are."

"Yeah," Bobby snarled. "But after this, they're gonna know how *we* are too!"

It was dusk, about time for capture-the-flag to begin. There were two small hills about three hundred yards apart just inside the woods. Atop each rise fluttered a flag—a blue one for the Watusis and a green one for the White-Eyes. But then the two teams added some minor alterations of their own. On their flag, the Watusis inked in a black clenched fist. On theirs, the White-Eyes sketched a white skull-and-crossbones.

The two teams gathered around their flags and on Hulk's whistle launched their actions to go for the opponents' flag.

The game proceeded in almost military fashion, first with cautious scouting and patrols around each other's perimeters, then with more daring probing actions.

To win, a team had not only to capture the opponents' flag, but to plant it on their own hilltop. The best way to achieve that was to make as many "captures" of opponents as possible to clear the way. All you had to do was touch an opponent and he was captured. First to go in this manner were the youngest and smallest, many of whom were nearly asleep.

Counselors, serving as umpires, skulked through the woods keeping an eye on likely captures.

Turkey Wingo sneaked up on Dogbreath. But at the last instant, Dogbreath saw him, shot him a bolt of disabling breath, and dashed off into the woods.

Pachuco Ortiz, one of the smallest orphans, who, although he pretended to violence, was a rabid lover of flowers, was sitting on the ground savoring the aroma of some night-blooming jasmine.

Charlie Stritzinger happened upon him and, startled by the sight, stood gaping.

Pachuco looked up in embarrassment. "Smells good."

"I hate flowers!" Charlie snapped, stomping the jasmine. Then the two grappled, both claiming a capture.

"Charlie got you, Pachuco," Vance announced.

Dee Dee spent most of her time lingering near their flag, keeping an eye on Bobby Stenzel, who appeared from time to time after a foray, strutting like John Wayne as he delivered captives to their base.

"Handsome," Dianne whispered.

"Okay, that's all," Dee Dee answered.

A White-Eyed patrol tried a frontal attack on the Watusi hill and was repulsed, scattering into the woods. Charlie and Robin eluded their pursuers, then flopped together on the ground under some brush, panting like crazy.

"Pooped," she gasped.

"Me too."

"Did you see the capture Bad Henry made on Gale?

Nearly slugged him. Who cares who wins this stupid game?"

"Well—"

"I don't want camp to end," she said softly.

"Me neither. But we'll be back next year, right?"

"Yeah," she said, brightening. "Will you and I, will we still, um—"

"Yeah." He blushed.

"Where the devil is everybody?" came the yell from Bobby Stenzel, who was beating through the underbrush trying to rally his troops.

Robin and Charlie got up quickly, just as he appeared in front of them.

"Come on, let's get with it!" Bobby snapped.

"We were chasing somebody."

They all ran off toward the Watusi hill.

Gradually the careful patrols were abandoned in favor of all-out frontal attacks by both sides.

"No defense," Luscious yelled to his team, "all offense!"

"Everybody charges!" commanded Bobby.

Both groups thrashed through the woods, yelling and capturing and advancing on the opposing flags. Boys swore and girls screeched, girls swore and boys screeched.

Bobby and Clarke broke through to the Watusi hilltop and charged for the flag.

It was gone.

At the same time, Luscious and Bad Henry and Sateen clambered to the White-Eye hilltop and lunged for where the flag should be.

It too was gone.

On either hilltop, the opposing forces milled around in confusion.

"You got no flag up here, you cheaters!" Bobby bellowed back toward his own hilltop.

"Don't call us cheaters!" Luscious answered, cupping his hands around his mouth. "Somebody musta *ate* your flag! Probably *you*, Stenzel!"

The two teams charged down off the hilltops and met halfway between, issuing charges and counter-charges and threats and denials.

Then, spent, they stood staring at each other, gasping for breath, searching for words.

"Well, there ain't no flags," Luscious growled, stepping up to Bobby.

"Well, then there ain't no darned *game!*" Bobby snarled back, squaring off against him, toe to toe.

"So?"

"So?"

"So!" Bobby turned on his heel and led his forces out of the woods back in the direction of the council ring.

"So." Luscious waved his army forward, and they followed.

Steamboat was awaiting their arrival. He stood somberly in the center of the ring, arms folded across his broad chest.

They trooped in, exhausted and grumbling, flopped down onto their logs, slapped their thighs angrily, and stared at the fire.

"Everybody's in," Hulk said.

Steamboat nodded and looked over the disheartened, disappointed, disgruntled campers.

Now, from under his shirt, he pulled out the two flags and held them up.

Campers gaped.

"Yes, boys and girls, here they are." He waved the flags in either hand. "Nobody won Field Day."

There were some scattered moans and sighs.

"But then, *everybody* won Field Day, too. You were right, and I was right. I won. You won."

There were a few more groans and mutterings, a bit louder.

"And here's why." Steamboat began pacing around the ring, looking into the face of each camper. "In camp you're supposed to learn a little bit about life. Just like everywhere else. Well, one of the things about life is that no matter how hard you strive for something, how hard you fight for a flag or pull a rope or try to win a game, somebody bigger than you are can come along and beat you. You can always have some victories, but there's always somebody else who can take them away."

He stopped pacing right in front of Piano Legs and looked into his eyes. "You're never going to win all the time. Somebody can always take something away from you. But then, sometimes somebody comes along and gives it back to you. It happens to all of you. And it happens to me."

Piano Legs closed his eyes, smiling slightly.

"Now, competition is a healthy thing, a normal and productive thing. But winning at any cost isn't. Because if you win at too high a cost, you're going to lose at too high a cost too. My football team went one-and-eight last year because I think it ought to be fun instead of so darned important—and there were ways we prepared for and played the games that avoided some of the harmful, destructive things other teams do. It's the same way here at this camp. Always has been, always will be, so long as I'm around."

He resumed his pacing. "So this particular war is over. Here!" He tossed one flag to Luscious, the other to Bobby. "Now everybody join hands. Come on, right here around the ring. I mean *everybody!*"

Reluctantly at first, then more willingly, then gladly, the campers pushed in together and reached for hands. Orphans mixed with old campers. As they touched, the tension seemed magically to drain from the area.

"Good. Now, sing!" In his rolling baritone, Steamboat began the camp song: "You can't be blue at Smilin' Through . . ."

And by the time he had finished a couple of bars, the group was singing. It spread as if contagious, first the voices of the old campers, then filled in by the orphans who quickly caught the repeated words. Their voices rose individually, then filled the camp. By the last bars, they were all singing at the tops of their lungs.

Then it was over, and they were again nearly breathless from the effort.

Luscious Moncrief and Bobby Stenzel found themselves face-to-face.

"Just wait till next year, man," Luscious said, fixing him with a stern look.

"I'll be here, man," Bobby responded.

Then, with neither of them relinquishing their fierce stares, the two slapped palms loudly with each other.

The camp erupted in a mighty, spontaneous cheer.

The three yellow charter buses pulled into the parking lot, their drivers wheezing like the dying engines as the men scanned unhappily the happy, loud campers milling boisterously around their duffel bags.

Orphans and old campers mingled to say their farewells, slapping palms, issuing challenges for next year, exchanging addresses and phone numbers.

Steamboat called for quiet. Gradually they directed their attention to him. "It's been an unforgettable summer. But everything came out right, in my opinion. A good camp is proven by the good-byes among the campers, and I see plenty to be proud of all around me!"

Vance stepped in front of him, facing the campers. "But two more things, though," he said. "We never got Steamboat on a skateboard, and we never got the all-time great kamikaze I dreamed about this year! I promised you camp would not end without that!"

All heads turned toward Steamboat.

"Aw, well . . ." Steamboat shrugged his shoulders

and looked toward the asphalt walk. "Who's got a skateboard?"

Clark Brunkhorst hauled his board out of his bag and held it out.

Steamboat took it and looked it over.

"Careful now, Steamboat," Clark said. "It's the fastest board in the West. It can get away from you."

"Anything a kid can do," Steamboat said, cradling the board and stalking over to the walk, "I can do."

He stepped onto the board, and it immediately skittered out from under him, sending him stumbling from the walk.

Clark caught the board.

"Gimme it!" This time Steamboat managed to steady himself aboard, teetering, as he took off down the walk.

"Go, Steamboat!"

"Go, go, go!"

As the kids ran alongside hollering encouragment, Steamboat, licking his lips, picked up speed. As he went faster and faster, he began to yell. As he zipped onto the dock, the yell became his fullest Tarzan bellow.

"Aaaaeeeeyaaa!" Then, at the end of the dock, he was launched. High into the air he soared, tumbling. He turned one lofty somersault, two, two and a half. Waving his arms and legs, he hit the water flat on his stomach with a splash that rose twenty feet into the air.

And then, right behind him, on his own board, came Piano Legs. He sailed almost as high as Steamboat, and almost as far, yelling almost as loud, landing with a second splat in the water right beside him.

"The ultimate kamikaze!" Vance screamed ecstatically. "Two of them!"

There was a brief hush as the campers waited for them to surface.

Then, to the accompaniment of a cheer that

reached a deafening pitch, father and son bobbed up, raising linked hands high into the air.

"Welcome to Camp Washakie!" the pair roared together.

"Simply one of the best novels written for any age group this year."—*Newsweek*

I AM THE CHEESE

BY **ROBERT CORMIER**
AUTHOR OF <u>THE CHOCOLATE WAR</u>

Adam Farmer is a teenager on a suspenseful quest, at once an arduous journey by bicycle to find his father and a desperate investigation into the mysteries of the mind. What exactly is Adam looking for? Where is his father? Why does he have two birth certificates? What is the meaning of his parents' whispered conferences? Of their sudden move to a new town? Of his mother's secret Thursday afternoon phone calls? Of the strange man who appears and reappears in their lives? And why are Adam's thoughts constantly interrupted by an unidentified interrogator who prods him to recall some recent, devastating catastrophe? "The secret, revealed at the end, explodes like an H-bomb."—*Publishers Weekly*

Laurel-Leaf Library $1.50

At your local bookstore or use this handy coupon for ordering:

| **Dell** | **DELL BOOKS**
 P.O. BOX 1000, PINEBROOK, N.J. 07058 | I Am The Cheese $1.50 (94060-5) |

Please send me the above title. I am enclosing $_____
(please add 35¢ per copy to cover postage and handling). Send check or money order—no cash or C.O.D.'s. Please allow up to 8 weeks for shipment.

Mr/Mrs/Miss_____

Address_____

City_____ State/Zip_____